D0406132

Love and Fatigue in America

Terrace Books, a trade imprint of the University of Wisconsin Press,
takes its name from the Memorial Union Terrace, located at
the University of Wisconsin–Madison. Since its inception in 1907,
the Wisconsin Union has provided a venue for students, faculty, staff, and
alumni to debate art, music, politics, and the issues of the day. It is a place
where theater, music, drama, literature, dance, outdoor activities, and
major speakers are made available to the campus and the community.
To learn more about the Union, visit www.union.wisc.edu.

Love and Fatigue in America

Roger King

Terrace Books

A Trade imprint of the University of Wisconsin Press

Terrace Books
A trade imprint of the University of Wisconsin Press
1930 Monroe Street, 3rd Floor
Madison, Wisconsin 53711-2059
uwpress.wisc.edu

3 Henrietta Street
London WCE 8LU, England
eurospanbookstore.com

Printed in the United States of America

Library of Congress Cataloging-in-Publication Data
King, Roger, 1947–
Love and fatigue in America / Roger King.
p. cm.
ISBN 978-0-299-28720-7 (cloth: alk. paper)
ISBN 978-0-299-28723-8 (e-book)
1. King, Roger, 1947–
2. Chronic fatigue syndrome—Patients—Biography.
I. Title.
PR6061.I473Z46 2012
823′.914—dc23
[B]
2011042648

To D.S.

Contents

Author's Note

At first glance the autobiographical novel, despite a distinguished history, is a slippery genre, an apparent oxymoron claiming both the authority of fact and the freedom of fiction. A clarification might be called for.

The events in this book are, as far as I am able to recollect, true in time and place and in my experience of them, though the experience is necessarily subjective and is filtered through the voice of the nameless narrator. Any insights that might accumulate through the book have these recollections as their foundation.

This leaves untouched the apparent contradiction that any novel is by definition fiction. But within this contradiction there is contained a subtle truth: that memoir is always a reimagined past and never literal, and that fiction is never fully imagined, even though its license in more literary.

The act of recall in the brain is, it is now widely thought, indistinguishable from the act of imagining, and we fool not just others but ourselves if we insist that our latest memory is a simple retrieval of the past. In the particular case of *Love and Fatigue in America*, this universal truth of the fallibility of reimagined memory is further complicated by a narrator suffering from a neurological illness that undermines the formation of new memories, as well as later access to them. This peculiarity is overtly part of the story, its content, and its shifting, fragmented form.

While the narrator must be, in my choosing his voice and tone, a character not fully myself, the other characters in the book are more definitively fictional characters in a novel. Not only are they subjectively portrayed by a narrator straining for reliability, but also names and the circumstantial details of lives have been deliberately altered to conceal and protect the identities of the original inspirers. This novelistic freedom does not, I hope, distort the essentials of their stories, which require essential reliability to claim for the book a complex truth soundly drawn from life, an autobiographical novel.

Washington State, 1990–1991

How to Arrive

It could almost be Pakistan's North-West Frontier, with the mountains over there, but it's the Rockies not the Hindu Kush. From this height, the endless forests to the north could be—if I squint to confuse pines with palms—those of Liberia or Sierra Leone. Except there are no dotted village clearings. There are hardly any signs of humans at all, just the one brave, straight road and the occasional bald hilltop, in shock from clear-cut logging. Looks like forestry might be the main industry down there.

The plane is circling. I've done this often, flown into new places with a job to do. I've learned to sum things up before even setting foot. Actually, I think I'm good at this, arriving.

And that must be Spokane, the center around which we're turning, the designated location of my new life. An isolated city. Judging from the way it spreads out along the valleys, land must be cheap. Not many cities look like this. They tend to be crammed, or tall, or both. The highest buildings in downtown Spokane are unconvincing, an urban idea borrowed from other places where it was more necessary. It's small as cities go—say, one or two hundred thousand—but it's by far the biggest place in our wide view. So, there it is, I've clocked it: a small isolated city serving a vast, sparsely populated hinterland.

As foreign cities go, this one should be easy. I smile at the window, recognizing something of my foolishness in this thought. Of course, they'll think their city is the center of the world, everyone does. But after Beijing, Lagos—London, even—it's just a town, and its simplicity will be relaxing. They even speak English. I'm hoping it will be easy, and its people easy to impress, since I'm anxious about this new job, teaching graduate students subjects I've never studied. The truth is I've always been nervous about teaching—the inescapable prominence of the teacher in the classroom—but I believe this fear ridiculous at my age, and squelch it. I've closed my copy of *Jane Eyre*, now the scene below has my attention. There's no need to mark the place. Its pages are grizzled up to page 190 with the deep scorings I've made all the way from London.

Never mind the anxiety, we're west of the city now and the land is dry, almost desert: few trees and not much potential for farming. "Badlands"—I think that's the American term for it. There are few settlements but then you can tell there isn't enough water to support more. Out of habit, I've been checking the rivers to estimate the possibilities for irrigation. Before I put *Jane Eyre* on the reading list, I really should have read it. I thought I had, but none of it seems familiar. But this is good, isn't it, a new job, a new challenge, a whole new life at forty-three?

It's what I've always done, setting myself up for new tests in new places and then trusting on adrenaline to see me through, using the fear of public failure to overcome a tendency to shy away from life into dream. So far it's worked. The encyclopedia said Spokane is known as the capital of the Inland Empire. The dryness could be a rain shadow from the coastal mountains, which I can just make out from here.

Four weeks was the time usually allowed me by U.N. agencies for a new African or Asian country, to comprehend its people and its problems, propose a solution. Madness, of course, a new country every few months, and an understanding that was all effort and mind. I've been writing about the falseness of it, and it's time to walk away from this in favor of integrity and this new life. Apparently,

I'll be part of the Department of Humanities at Inland University. It sounds lovely, the Humanities. I wonder who I will meet down there and whether someone will surprise me.

The beginning of this journey could not have been more promising: an invitation out of the blue, perfectly timed. A poet in Spokane called my London flat and asked if I might be interested in visiting for a year, teaching creative writing, literature and film at Inland University, where he worked. I had never taught any of these, nor had I heard of him, the university, or Spokane, yet the offer immediately seemed just right.

I thought it possible that he was mistaking me for someone else. I had not once encountered any stranger who had read my books.

It happened once before, an inexplicable offer out of the blue. Then I had been living in London too, at twenty-five, working in a pub, when a fat envelope containing a contract from the Nigerian government plopped onto my doormat without explanation. If I signed it I would be teaching agricultural economics at a Nigerian university I had not heard of. I signed, booked a plane, and it had made my life up to now: an expert on rural poverty and the author of novels set in West Africa. It had worked out well, I thought, the hand of fate.

Now, for complicated reasons, I was again eager to leave London, and again there was an inexplicable, perfect offer. America was where I wanted to go. The poet cautiously revealed that my responsibilities might be arduous, and I cautiously revealed that my doctorate was in agricultural economics, not English literature, and that my last job assignment had been in Chinese Inner Mongolia, to do with livestock. I heard him falter, then assert that this might be OK, good even, that his students were too sheltered and would benefit from something new.

I was to call him back in two days, but before I put down the phone I already knew I would accept, and that when the year was up I would stay in America. I smiled at my luck, and went to find Spokane in the atlas.

It's different again to the south: rolling hills of golden grain and black plowed earth. This is rich farmland. I can tell from the tidy farm buildings and farmhouses, and the little space they allow themselves, that it is a prosperous, modern agriculture where land is valuable. They must be beyond the rain shadow here. That rich soil might have been left behind by retreating glaciers, or perhaps a prehistoric flood. Geology makes settlements, makes economics, makes culture, makes us what we are. It's the big picture. The plane window picture.

My new life will not be like my old life. In this new life I'll have one career not two. I'll stay in one place, live with one woman. I'll be undivided and whole. I'll put the recent difficulties of London behind me quickly with the accelerated forgetting offered by distance. I'll make love work down there; it's not too late. I'll settle, be a settler. There will be no to-ing and fro-ing in love for fifteen years, as there had been with my Indian girlfriend. Suddenly I'm overwhelmed by feelings for her, which I push down and away, feeling the push back at me from this compression of history. But I can't solve that old puzzle now. It's another reason to move on. For her good as much as mine. Still, I suspect I am a fool; I'm just unclear what sort of fool.

I have an idea about love for after I've landed. Well, two ideas really, which on the face of things is one too many, but since I am flying and fleeing, I am large with possibility and above contradiction. My first and most exciting idea is the young woman from New York, who, suitably for a new life, is recently met and, appropriately for renewal, significantly younger. We will both be, I can argue, in our different ways, just starting out. She's an artist, serious, talented, struggling, and as she asserts, cute, and as she also asserts, a dirty-blonde—an American term new to me which I've learned refers to hair color, not an intriguing moral laxity. She's the daughter of Mennonite missionaries and is not lax. She has never lived with a man, but thinks she could use a home, and love. We don't know each other well—but this seems right for a new life too. I can see the future: a lively, prosperous partnership, dedicated to great work and beloved children.

But I've also gained the impression from the novels of older Englishmen, David Lodge and others, that the actual teaching of writing in America generally takes second place to drunken parties and the liberation from our native reserve offered by sexually insistent students. So, that's my second idea about love, in case the girlfriend from New York falls through. I shouldn't let myself think of these other, unknown women, but since I am, it is true that I don't actually know when she is arriving from New York, or for certain that she will, so technically I am perhaps still single. All the possible outcomes are good. I'm fit; I'm in motion; the past is history.

In the air, success seems inevitable. I'm descending on America. I'm full of untapped energy. My new, uncompleted novel already has a New York publisher, an advance, and a deadline. The BBC in London wants a screenplay from me. Things are moving. There's this job. There's the promising girlfriend.

Here's Spokane coming around again. There's nothing to stop its spread that I can see, except the urge of people to be close. It made sense to seed a city here, on a big river, a market center for the forests up into Canada and the farms down to Oregon. There seem to be two airports, one military and the one we're heading for. And there's one huge factory outside of town, its sign now visible at this height—Kaiser Aluminum, a smelter. Well, that's probably here to exploit the snowmelt water flowing from the Rockies

I close my eyes for a long moment, then open them. You know what? I don't have to do this anymore. I can let the geology and the economics go. My interest now, as we go low, is in those mysterious rows of houses, the unknown people in them—perhaps new friends—not the region's economic prospects. I no longer need to visit government officials while carrying a heavy briefcase, or listen for hours to the rural poor, or analyze social structure with a busy mind. My interest now is in those streets, their bars and cafes, my new colleagues, the students, the unknown ways I'll be drawn by America into involvement and belonging. I only need to accept the invitation and relax. There's the squeal of a small animal as we touch down.

There Is This about Love

There is this about love: it is a puzzle.

I love readily and well
I listen
I adore
I am ready with practical solutions to life's problems
I am there with sympathy
I am good in emergencies, and generous
I am playful
I like to talk
I do not shy away from difficulties
I like the quiet times of reading together in bed
I am good at being a couple in company
I am funny
I am aware of the need for equality in domestic labor
I am warm
I am sensual
I am fascinated by women's bodies
I am patient at bringing them to orgasm
I am tender in the aftermath
I am easy with women, friendly
I look at new ones, wonder about them
I see in the one I have fresh imperfections
An unbecoming angle, a social tic
I am oppressed by calls on me
To give where I do not want to give

I move away
I blame myself for blaming
I love, but cannot stay
It is unbearable
I am gone
In absence, the panic falls from me
Leaving loneliness
I love most of all the imperfections then
For the humanity in them
I am incomplete with love unexpressed.
I negotiate, return, come to terms, see sense
I stay
Until the tension proves again that sense is not, after all
Of the essence.

There is this about love: I am good at it.

There is this about love: I am bad at it.

I have been, in love, the puzzle piece that completes the picture by losing itself
Useless when separate
Without existence when joined.

Home I: Cabin in Spokane

Got away, got away with it.

I am sitting, this October evening, on the cabin's rough-wood balcony, my feet up on the rail, watching the day fade over the Little Spokane River below me. Deer mooch in the yard, then leap the fence silently, on a whim. I smoke a rare cigarette and feel content.

They put me in a modern apartment at first, but I held out for this wood cabin outside of town—more American—waiting for cautious Wayne, the landlord, to come to terms with my lack of a credit record. I'd never heard of credit records.

It's charming, this cabin, hand-built on a hillside, with a little bridge to an upstairs front door. Behind it, the land falls away steeply to the river so that the living room window and the balcony command a grand view. Tall pines shade it. There's not a single home like this in England. If it were not so obvious, I'd buy cowboy boots to prop up on the rail. As it is, I've bought a pickup, which looks just right, I think, parked on the dirt track to the door. Got away.

The classes are going well; the students like me. I'm working hard and productively. And the artist from New York says she'll join me here in a few weeks, bringing her art materials on the train.

Only two months out of London and my American life has fallen into place: the job, the cabin, the pickup, the girl. Got away with it.

The Fall

So, one day a man walks into a gym.

Tuesday, April 23, in fact.1991. An Englishman. The Sta-Fit gym. Spokane, Washington, U.S.A. 8 p.m.

I'm doing all right in this new life, seven months into it. Well, there was that bout of flu two weeks ago, but I'm over that. That's why I'm here tonight. To get back into shape.

And I haven't let the illness slow me down, finishing the new book to deadline in the midst of fever, exploiting the intensity. I've sent it off and prepared my classes for the new quarter too. I have, I think, done OK.

It's true that the girlfriend, the painter, the dirty blonde, has returned to New York, feeling out of place and neglected in Spokane. I did my best; it couldn't be helped. It's possible I'm heartbroken, but I haven't had time to know for sure.

My gym clothes are on the drab side compared with the other two in the weight circuit room: black swim shorts and tennis shoes held over from London. I haven't yet adopted the American custom of shopping for new costumes to match each new activity. The other two have. The male has one of those skinny weight-lifting vests over a T-shirt, and a broad weight lifter's belt. The female's wearing shiny purple Spandex, making her bottom sleek as a seal's. We are the only three in the room, and no smile or greeting has been exchanged, creating that special gym tension of mutually denied awareness. We share the rock music.

I'm the oldest and the least fit. The other two are around thirty: she with a ponytail and attitude; he with a warrior stoniness. So, I'm doing my circuit, the leg raises, then the shoulder pulls. I'm surprised at how much the flu took out of me, that I'm having to notch the weights way down from where I was a month ago, but I stay cool and try not to let the others see I'm struggling. My muscles are lazy tonight, and I set about pushing them harder, as if they are not quite me. There was that thing I heard once, that you have to tear your muscles to build them.

I move on to the next station on the circuit, the simple step. Up down, up down, to get the heartbeat and the breathing going, a sort of respite between the hard stuff. But I'm finding it a strain. My heart is not playing the game. I give effort another kick, then I'm dizzy. I stand back, shaking my head to clear it. I shake my whole body as if to clear that too, shaking out tension, like an athlete. It's acceptable gym behavior. The trouble is, my eyesight is breaking up and a wave of wooziness is passing through me. The scene, the chromed machines, the teal walls with pink trim—the decade's favored colors for airports, hospitals and gyms—has gone kaleidoscopic, shot through with shifting jags of light. The shaking isn't helping.

I hang my head, imitating thought, and make my way slowly to where the wall last was, and find it. I slide down to the floor and adopt a rueful gym-appropriate grimace, giving a keen glance toward the others, as if I could actually see them. A dizzy spell. Well, it was stupid to overdo it the first time out after flu. I know that now. I'll wait it out, like a planned interlude between—what do the gym people call them?—yes, reps.

It's funny how the sitting down doesn't end the going down—like gravity does not know where to stop, and its giant hand persists in pushing on my shoulders, insisting I go right through the floor, or failing that, to be flattened on it like paint. I cannot let this happen. It would look bad. It might attract attention. I concentrate on the countervailing force offered by friction, back pressed against the wall, feet pulled up and flat on the carpet. I stare out with unseeing eyes—they are busy playing their own games of light and dark—a hint of a smile on my lips. Not ridiculous, I hope.

The pressing weight is enormous, too much for my muscles, which have themselves turned into dead weight. After receiving an urgent petition from the neck, I let my head drop. My heart has gone deep. It's beating down there, but very slowly. There's nothing to do but wait, I tell myself.

I have, after all, been dizzy before. There was that time in the parched bush of northern Nigeria. It was malaria and dehydration then, and three days unconscious as far as I could find out later. People I never met carried me to a bush clinic with no doctor. Others brought me food—rice, plantain, chicken—when I came to. I recovered, gained strength, carried on working. This is nothing like that. Here I'm surrounded by teal, pink, and shining chrome. I'm in Spokane, America, a country with many doctors. The other two are still clanking their machines. That's good.

It's quiet. I must be alone now. When did this happen? It is, perhaps, closing time. I want to be at home, flat on my bed. I do not want to be discovered here by the vain, pretty girl at the desk—compact as a battery in her official black shorts—who did not say hello. She'd just be annoyed at the trouble.

For no obvious reason my sight is coming back, the picture recomposing itself. There it is, an empty gym with just a few bolts of white light shooting through it. OK, this is it. I brace against the wall, push up with my arms, push back with my feet. I'm rising. I'm pushing at gravity and it's pushing back. Tough battle. But now I'm up. Still leaning, but up. Shaking a bit. Prudently, I keep my head down—why fight more than you have to? It's pretty high up here. It's a good distance down to the carpet. The carpet wants me.

Who knew standing was such a trick? The madness of it! Those feet; I'll never be able to balance on them. The body, by nature, wants to topple this way and that. It's not stable, so you have all these pulleys and pivots to check and balance it. I haven't realized until now what a complicated job it is. My muscles used to carry the burden. Now they are the burden. But, here goes. I'm moving. Pretty comic, I know, the way I'm swinging my legs instead of lifting them. And so slow. I only need to make it to my pickup parked outside the door. Only a mile to drive to bed.

As I slowly move past the girl at the reception desk, who is making a point of not looking at me, I try for normality. I'm even saying something. There's a ghastly sound that must be me. The girl is looking now, following my unnatural progress toward the door. What is that expression on her face? It's not exactly surprise . . . it's more like horror.

To myself, I say: a good night's rest and you'll be right tomorrow.

Doctor I: Grumpy

The morning after I collapsed at the gym I am not, after all, better. Two weeks later I am still not better, and it's time to see a doctor.

The doctor I have in mind is the one closest to my cabin. I've passed his roadside sign each time I've driven into town. It's one of those glass cabinet signs that are most commonly found outside Spokane's startlingly numerous churches, which include the converted supermarket near my home, now a big box of Baptists. Rather than little bits of scripture, aphorism, or threat, the doctor's sign simply bears his name and, Family Practice.

The waiting room is empty and the reading matter on its tables undisturbed. The receptionist concedes that the doctor can see me now.

He's in a white coat, standing behind his desk, occupied with moving sample medicines from his drawer to shelves, or vice versa, in any case not acknowledging my presence, fiddling while I burn. When he does turn, the furious glare on his gray, quilted face indicates that I've importuned him in the course of more important business. Unable to stand, I surrender to a chair and see him flinch at this new affront.

"Symptoms?" he asks, at last, and I articulate as best I can the experience of the last two weeks: the dizziness, the refusal of my brain to perform or my muscles to respond, the swollen glands, the diarrhea, sore throat, sleeplessness, aching head, everything crazy and awry. Viewed from behind his glinting glasses, my claims are clearly preposterous.

Perhaps this grumpy man has problems of his own, a deep-seated, blameless incapacity for social interaction, a family tragedy, a minor autism, an absent gene for charm and conversation. He says nothing in response to my weak attempts at articulating the shifting elements of my complaint, except, "Take these to reception," handing me some papers on which he has summarily scribbled. I try to read them, but he folds them away from me, repeating, "To reception."

I take the receptionist to be his wife, a thin elderly woman tight with misery and apparently sworn to secrecy. I glimpse, though, what he's written: "Flu symptoms."
She hands me back my health insurance card and credit card and, with them, a receipt, an order form in triplicate for a lab—"They'll take your blood"—and a sheaf of forms for me to complete right away, now, in the empty waiting room, before I leave.

This is all strange to me. In England, served by the National Health Service, I grew up with hands-in-your-pockets health care. I walked into doctors' surgeries without papers and walked out without papers, doing nothing with papers in between. No money changed hands. The doctor had my records or could get them, organized my further tests and consultations, and was not concerned by my income or his. Papers were the doctor's business; the patient's business was to be sick.

Grumpy, I learn, has recently arrived from Canada. My guess is that he left because of a scandal involving malpractice, sexual impropriety or, at the very least, an apoplectic distaste for socialized medicine. He's old and his practice is unpopular. There's a mad defensiveness about him. If money was his motive for coming, things look bad.

On my follow-up visit, he announces: "You have chronic fatigue syndrome."
I've never heard of this, and wait.
"It's called ME disease in Canada. No doubt in England too."
I've not heard of that either, and wait.
"Myalgic encephalomyelitis," he says.
I wait again but nothing more is forthcoming. "Is it," I ask, "serious?"
"You don't die."
"Ah."
Grumpy is becoming agitated by this idle chitchat, growing pinkly furious, to evade which he addresses the lab results. "Your Epstein-Barr antibodies are elevated. Exceptionally elevated. Chronic fatigue syndrome is the result of the Epstein-Barr virus."

I feel there should be more. I ask my addled and reluctant brain to think about what more might be, and at last it comes up with something: "How long does it last?"
"Years. Maybe forever."
"Forever?"
With a pained hint of compassion, he concedes, "Some people seem to recover." Then, in retreat from this, "Some get worse."

I sit in blank and immobile silence, a state I rather like for its own sake. There is something else I should ask, I'm sure, but my brain comes up with nothing. Ah, yes, "What's the treatment?"
"There's no treatment." A pause. "Rest. Eat sensibly."

And here are the papers, again pushed across the desk in dismissal. I am still trying to think, and since standing and thinking are separately difficult but simultaneously impossible, I stay sitting. And since I have not moved to leave, he does, abruptly opening the door behind his desk and bolting through it.

There is something wrong here, something unsatisfactory. In retrospect, it must be that I have just been assigned a lifetime of

comprehensively disabling illness without hope or treatment, but at the time I can't quite identify the problem.
"How did I catch it?" I manage, to his departing back.
"Nobody knows," he throws back over his shoulder, as the door closes.
He's gone.

Early Days

Interesting this, getting beaten up by a rag-tag gang of misfit symptoms, which is now the content of my days. I struggle to my feet, stagger a few steps, and they knock me down again. There's the dizziness, and the heart going slow, falling down on its job of keeping the blood rushing around. Then there's this puzzling refusal of the legs to tense and flex according to instructions. The muscles are just dead meat; meat with a little singing tingle deep inside, a whirr of disengagement. My brain is offal, bloated, soft, pressing achingly against my skull, the antithesis of mental sharpness. It can't remember, won't decide, is irritated. The lymph glands are swollen, the eyes will not focus. It's a great effort to sit up, almost impossible to stand. There's the insomnia and the diarrhea, the repeated urinations, the pain in every joint. It's all disarray. A madman has seized the controls. What it does not resemble in any way is the mild and sloppy word "fatigue."

When, as mysteriously as their appearance, the symptoms temporarily slink back into the shadows, I am left beaten up and washed out but more or less my old self, my mind returned to me. With each remission I am convinced that the recovery will be permanent, and each time I am proved wrong. This never changes. Health is unable to imagine being ill; illness cannot recall a state of health.

I now hear anecdotes about other sufferers from chronic fatigue syndrome, or CFS. One woman, I am told, went to bed, dosed herself with vitamins, and, after six months of rest, got up again, completely recovered. I am certain that I will be well before six months. And I cannot even consider taking to my bed, since I have a new life to make. A second woman, a graduate student, has reputedly suffered from CFS for seven years, but I can't believe she has the same illness as me. Or, if she has, I assume she must possess a weaker disposition. Mine, I assert to myself, is positive, optimistic, able, not that of a victim. I recover quickly from illnesses. I know this because I had lots of them in Africa, sometimes treated with antibiotics I bought from roadside stalls. This one should be nothing. And then, I'm lucky. Luck is on my side.

On the best days I make guest appearances at my own classes, leaving again before I lose the ability to drive home. My nine-month contract is nearly done. The film class watches films and writes screenplays according to my class plan, with the cooperative graduate students taking turns to lead discussions. For the undergraduate class I depend on two teaching assistants, Carol and Dean, both eager to prove themselves. Carol volunteers to take a bus to deliver the student papers to me.

I call the poet who first invited me to Spokane to tell him that I am missing classes because of a mystifying illness. He tells me to do my best, offering no help. I reply that I will, relieved that so early a failure in my new life might be so easily overlooked. My other colleagues are entirely silent, each terrified that he or she might be asked to take on extra work. In fact, I've hardly seen my colleagues since I first arrived at Inland University, which turns out to be more a vacant space for educational brief encounters than a community of scholars. Teaching resembles feeding time at the zoo: wary professors slipping in from home to toss classes to the students, then running away before they can be caught.

My unpaid bills are piled up along the back of the tweedy couch that is now my daytime home. I've written one check today and the envelope containing it is on the floor next to a pile of unread student papers. That will do for now. I am hoping that dealing with one bill a day will be sufficient, though the pile of envelopes from doctors, laboratories, and health insurers still seems to be growing.

The second pile of envelopes—the personal letters of a pre-email era—is entirely untouched. I always intend to get to these letters after I've achieved the necessities of the day, but I never achieve these necessities. The letters are from around the world, all the places where I've lived or worked and made good friends. When the local post office held my mail, the clerk commended me on all this foreignness, and I've been saving the stamps for his son. I see that the top letter, the last of a wonderful decade-long exchange with a scandalously witty woman from Zanzibar, already has a thin covering of dust. This pile has gone dry and hopeless now that I no longer reply to anyone. I can hear the hiss of a receding tide, as the world gives up on me.

It's time to urinate again, a too frequent expedition from the couch to the bathroom. It's a humble thing these days, urinating. I no longer stand. When I reach the toilet I'm grateful to sit like a woman, and in any case the stream does not justify the stance. I no longer piss, I drain. All force has been lost. Apparently, my bladder muscles are as feeble as all the others. Making it back to the couch, I lie knocked out for half an hour, recovering from the big trip across the living room.

Wanting to be concerned for someone other than myself, I call my mother. I find there are only certain people I can call. These are mostly women, and then only certain women, because only they have the custom of talking at length with little requirement for my response. My mother, the original of this type, is always eager to pour into my ear the limitless detail of her life. It's a life of high narrative drama, full of "she said . . . " and "so, I said. . . ." and "you know what she's like." She has her complaints: the world is not fair, added to which her son is not just down the road like the sons of all her friends, does not have a nice wife like them, has not provided grandchildren, which are her due, all of which, she asserts, would make her son happy too, not like a life in America, which everyone knows is the ruin of down-to-earth English people. I'm lying on my side, the receiver balanced on my face to save the effort of holding it. Her talk weaves its sentences, chain-linked with "ands" and "buts," and breaths taken midsentence to discourage interruption.

It's an old, familiar voice saying old, familiar things, and I let its intimacy wash over me. Still, it is not all relaxation, there are insinuations to resist, including the repeated insistence that "we're just alike, you and me" and must be in league together against the rest. Resisting the temptation to argue takes some effort but I can't afford the greater expenditure that would come with actual expression of dissent. I am being trained by illness into even temper. But now she has abruptly stopped, and there is: "And how are you?" followed by a silence. "Oh, me?" I say, "I'm fine. Well, a bit under the weather. Actually, I'm resting." And she tells me vigorously that I must not do too much, and must not let people take advantage of me, because that's what happens to good-natured, generous people like me, and her.

The final weeks of my contract with Inland University play out. From my headquarters on the couch, I hand the final student grades to Carol, my teaching assistant. It's over. I am forgotten. The days lying down alone now seem longer, and the strings of days lying alone have a scouring loneliness. Yet I do have occasional visitors. They are my landlord, Wayne, who drops by biweekly to collect the rent, and, in sequence, over the next six months, I am visited by three women I first met before I fell ill. They are the last friends I will make who knew me as my healthy self. Without exception, my male ex-colleagues are made awkward by illness, and stay silent, and away.

There is something in my new stillness and quiet that nurtures intimacy. My visitors fill the space with their talk, relieving me of effort. In the presence of my weakness, they are inclined to offer their own. Hurt attracts hurt.

Army I: Krissy

Krissy visits me at the cabin, carrying a pie, which she holds aloft on her finger tips. "OK," she jokes, "you can have the pie, or me. Or both." She's breezy, sexy, reckless, kind. She was once a high jumper and still has a way of moving on her toes as if she might leap at any moment. But I'm stuck flat on the couch and Krissy looms above me, a giantess holding the pie high, like Liberty's torch. We live in different universes, the force of gravity all in mine.

When I first saw her, just after my arrival in Spokane, Krissy was laughing. It was her ringing laugh that made me turn and notice her at the party to introduce me to the English department. She was helpless in it, bending from the waist, a woman in her mid-thirties, long hair hanging, body loose. When she returned to upright, glowing, she caught my look. "I'm Krissy," she said, offering a straight arm. "I teach English as a foreign language." Her posture was excellent, athletic, now she was upright. There was an openness to her. She was healthy. We were both healthy.

I told her in answer to her questions that I was waiting for the arrival of my girlfriend from New York, who I was not entirely sure would arrive. "So," she joked, "are you looking for insurance?" Her manner was tipsy, but she was drinking water.

Now, nine months later, Krissy sits on the edge of my couch and talks, relieving me of the effort of conversation. The pie on her plate remains untouched. She was, it emerges, born in Spokane.

She joined the army at nineteen because she wanted her father to love her as much as he did his sons.

She says, of the U.S. Army, "You wouldn't believe how incompetent they are. How much they waste." She's no time for their bullshit now, she says.

She was sent, went, to Germany. A private. Cruised through the physical ordeals. For a willing, pretty nineteen-year-old girl, there was lots of sex, she says. She laughs, remembering this.

They taught her to drink, she says.
Her superior dealt her heroin.
Her superior turned her in for doing drugs when he was taking heat.
The military police investigated her. "We called them Buddy Fuckers," she says.
She conned the Buddy Fuckers, always carrying a vial of an abstemious friend's urine tucked into her underwear, in case of spot checks. She laughs at this too: her cheek; their stupidity.

There's a downhill heedlessness in the way Krissy holds nothing back.

She came to, alone one morning, in a German potato field, stripped, a bloody Buddy Fucker's baton lying next to her. She thinks she might have been unconscious from drink before they raped her, but isn't sure. She only knows for sure that it ended with her unconscious in a potato field, injured inside and out, bleeding from her rectum.

She has rushed so quickly to this humiliation that I feel that my quiet is a well into which she has flung herself. Such energy as I have is all concentrated into my attention to Krissy, and I reach out to hold her hand, though she may have forgotten me. She comes to, and says, "I guess I was too easy in those days." Then she adds her standing joke, "But you can have me if you like."

She left the army, because of the drugs, the rapes, the incompetence. An honorable discharge. Clean now. Six years and counting, she says. AA three times a week and a tight rein. She was not, after all, tipsy when I met her, not reckless. Just loose limbed.

On a later visit I watch Krissy as she walks from her old Volkswagen to my front door, some baked treat in her hand. Her stride is easy but her head is down, her face darkened by the shadow from her hair. When I open the door, she smiles, but I'm not convinced. It turns out that she's rattled by the Gulf War fervor now sweeping Spokane. The belligerent patriotism and glorification of the military are roiling her memories of the army. "I want out of here," she says. "My family, the people here, they love this war. They're dying to kill some foreigners. Whatever made you come here?"

I say, trying for a bigger picture, that there's always a reason for leaving a place, to find out what is of it, and what is of you. And I tell her that, for me, Spokane is a new place, and it was England that had become a problem. I explain that London had become painful for me in a way, and I thought to find a new life here. "I needed to leave there," I tell her. "You need to leave here."

"Right." She hesitates, then, "What was it over there, exactly?"

"Well . . . there was some violence. Some trouble with the police . . ." I cannot be as open as Krissy about the tender places in me. "And—I told you—there was a relationship that did not work out."

"Right. Is that why you—you know—you don't seem that interested here?"

"Probably. I thought the Atlantic might help."

"Of course. You're unavailable. That must be why I like you. Has it helped, the Atlantic?"

"Not so far."

"So you're not much of a prospect?"

"Probably not. And, after all, I can barely stand."

"Well," she says, "I've got this chance to go to Russia. To teach English. Do you think I should take it? Or do you think I should stay?"

I say that Russia might be interesting these days, in 1991, the beginning of a whole new era. It could lead to something, a new career perhaps. She'd become an expert. "I'd think about going, if I were you," I say. "You're stuck here. Spokane's full of bad associations for you."

"You think?"

"Why not take the leap?"

"So, you won't be sorry to see me go?"

"Of course I'll be sorry. But I'll be moving too, as soon as I can."

"Shall I write?"

"Please do. Though I haven't been too good with letters recently."

Army II: Sucking on the Teat

"Spokane's sucking on the teat, all right," says Wayne the Baptist, "sucking on the teat of the military."

Wayne's my landlord, my age, glasses, a fussy moustache, soft voice, three kids. He always calls my cabin "the property," and he has a dozen other properties around the city, inherited from Dad.

Wayne is a devout Christian, a popular choice in Spokane, but he's open minded and wants to talk about everything with me. In particular, he's interested in the women who visit me. When he first met my girlfriend from New York, he looked at her with a wistful smile on his lips, as if he was imagining how it might be to be her lover instead of, say, a Baptist married with children. We were not having nearly as much fun as I imagined he imagined.

Wayne's wife disapproves of his visits to me and refuses to shake my hand. I assume this is in case I am the devil.

He's watchful and kind, and anyway prefers to have the rent placed directly into his palm. It's always the same: I lie down on the tweedy couch, my head on the armrest, and he remains standing, some distance from me. I can never persuade him to sit, though he often stays for an hour, talking me into exhaustion.

"Teat," in Wayne's mouth, is shocking. He has been moved to it by the Gulf War. Both he and I are against it, and in this we are bonded into a tiny and despised minority among the residents of Spokane, who turn out to be fierce warriors.

In the local papers and TV news, young mothers, dressed to kill, tenderly hold their babies in their camouflaged arms, ready to put them down to go to war. Some are in tears. More often it is the fathers going off to war, but sometimes the mother is the reservist, and sometimes young couples have taken a double share of military benefits, and it's both. Their government is unforgiving: they have taken the money, and now they must pay. I am fascinated and horrified by the tug-of-war between love and patriotism evident in this spectacle.

I tell Wayne that I had no idea that so many American families belonged to the military, that it went so deep. In Britain the army had registered as efficient, professional, low key, a slightly shameful, slightly suspect necessity, the sanitation workers of the nation-state. I knew no servicemen. Among my American friends—mostly East Coast academics—all the recent talk has been of the peace dividend offered by America's post–Cold War absence of enemies and a shrinking military. It was about new hope. Even Robert McNamara, the old hawk, has advocated cutting the military in half. But in Spokane the army seems to be not a regrettable necessity or a matter for intellectual debate, but an assumed part of family life, a long, happy, low-risk embrace.

It's when I make this observation that Wayne says the thing about Spokane sucking on the teat. "It isn't just the reservists," he explains. "There's the air force base and the contractors. It's what keeps the economy afloat. It's everywhere."

People, it is my impression, are generally pleased with themselves in Spokane. Its character is old-fashioned, industrious, cheery, self-contained, white. They are proud of its status as the capital of the Inland Empire, a mocked exemplar of the provincial. I've never visited anywhere with such friendly, chirpy shop assistants. The teased hair of young women drivers, observed from behind, surrounds their heads with halos of light.

Spokane life for men customarily involves the pleasure of machines: vintage cars, power boats for the lakes, snowmobiles, dirt bikes—a rambunctious internal combustion version of the outdoor life. A full-size pickup truck is the de rigueur prerequisite for this fullness.

They agree, the reservists, in television interviews, that it is their duty to go and fight the Iraqis, though their knowledge of where Kuwait is, or who the Iraqis are, is shaky. They appear to have no sense of what I know firsthand to be true, that the American government is widely loathed in poor countries around the world, nor do they seem to have any knowledge of the ruthless instances that have made this so. They know themselves to be nice.

There is pain. These young parents are perplexed to find that the demands of country and family, both under God, can be so at odds. Or that their government could be so harsh to those who love it.

"It's a tragedy," says Wayne.

"You know," I offer, from my prone position, eyes closed against the light, "it reminds me of *The Time Machine*. Do you know that book? H. G. Wells?" I open my eyes long enough to see Wayne shake his head. "Well, the hero arrives on his time machine at this delightful future civilization where everyone seems happy and prosperous, but not much interested in ideas. He can't understand how they support themselves and can't get anyone to talk about it. Then he discovers the ugly Morlocks who run the underground factories and provide everything to the nice people on the surface. They only ask for one thing in return. And that's that now and again they can come up at night and eat a few people."

Wayne looks at me blankly, then asks, "Is that by an English writer?"

"Yes. Look, it's sort of like the military reservists here, don't you think? The army provides a good life until it wants something. Then it insists on its payment. But, you know, for most people, most of the time, it seems like a good deal."

Wayne takes this in, then nods coolly and says that he supposes the stories might be considered similar in a way, but then adds sternly, "I'm not sure science fiction is helpful. America is a democracy."

I've been recklessly animated and Wayne's rebuke brings me back to the reality of my existence. "You're probably right," I say. "I'm feeling a bit tired now, Wayne."

America through the Ages

America at five
Is GI brides
Swept off their feet
By the money and big talk
Of its soldiers.
English housewives
My mother among them
Decried the brides
Low voiced through garden fences
And prophesied their ruin.

At nine, it was
The thick bright magazines
Passed on to us
By flashy Uncle Bob.
It's the fifties and we do not have
The things they show
A car, a phone, a fridge
Or any suchlike.
I study the glossy ads
And draw my young conclusion
That America is
The future.

From ten to eleven
And on

The English papers
Brighten our dim times
With the follies of Americans
Marrying at fifteen
Owning guns and shooting each other
Digging fallout shelters in their gardens
Gaining millions from nowhere and losing them
On childish fun
To be sad again.
We poor
Take comfort from America
That money makes you
Neither wise
Nor happy.

At twelve I can't sleep because of America. I see a BBC TV documentary proving that the unwise and callow Americans are ready to use nuclear weapons first, and might destroy us all. We decide the Americans are more frightening than their enemies, the Russians, who seem sad, stolid, resentful and slow—which we know to be adult qualities, and so less likely to lead us into destruction.

In my teens
The big deaths are American.
Kennedy
And Monroe.

As a student I visit America for the first time, selling encyclopedias door to door in Washington, DC, especially to military families. The pitch is a scam. People like my accent. I am unused to praise, or notice, or scams, and love Americans for their generosity. My boss tells me I am too polite to be effective and fires me. People, he says, let me talk just to hear me. I take off across the country on Greyhound buses.

My second woman ever
After the suburban student back home

Is a Hell's Angels girl
Met at the Flagstaff bus station.
She is sixteen and killing time
While her boyfriend is in jail.
She takes me home for sex
Then tricks me into shoplifting.
America is
I decide
Wide and open
And dangerous
And exciting.

I arrive in San Francisco during its crucial hippy summer
Nineteen sixty-seven
But am too shy to be part of it.
I come to no harm.

While washing dishes in a Seattle restaurant, I am invited by a famous American photographer to help with a photo shoot on the Crow reservation in Montana. He is the first artist I have ever met. Working with him—my job is talking to Crow families to distract them from his camera—I glimpse for the first time a mysterious and previously unsuspected form of happiness: the artist's loss of self-consciousness in his attention to the world. And America now stands for that, the grace of art.

I return from my summer in America changed, with cowboy boots and a false accent, feeling distinguished from my friends, and annoying them.

At twenty-two, I am in America again, to take up graduate studies in agriculture.

America is now
An older woman
Divorced
A psychologist

Who introduces me to
Intellectuals, artists, political activists
And says that I
Have something
So that I dare to think
Why not?
And America becomes
The holder of my young dreams.

At twenty-four America is
Antiwar demonstrations
In DC
And arguments for socialism
And free love.

During my thirties, America becomes gentle generosity, inviting me over from my work in England, Africa, and Asia to visit its artist colonies. I am offered comfortable lodging, inspiring company, and the assertion that I belong among them. I gain the peculiar impression that America honors the arts and cossets its artists.

At forty I am convinced that
I need America again
For all it has been to me
Through the ages
And so when
At forty-three
It issues an invitation out of the blue
I know
I must accept.

What Is Kind

I've been learning what is kind. Not supermarkets, it seems. And not action films, or antic comedies. Not TV, for the busy way it switches focus and subject. These send my neurons into disarray.

My injured self rather likes human faces and distant landscapes. Beauty, I suppose. It favors films about slowly shifting relationships that deepen as the story progresses. French films are often the kindest, and I've developed a taste for Eric Rohmer, whose gentle films I previously thought slight, but which now seem the most profound. I cannot afford to entertain violence, or fantasies of power, or manic glee, those nervous energies. My damaged brain seeks the patterns of early happiness, the human face, the human story, just as my faltering body cries out for the comfort and warmth of early nurture.

But even kindly films take their toll, even watched supine in bed. My new delight is to lie on my back for hours, perfectly still, eyes open but unfocused, muscles lax, doing . . . nothing. Stunned by the effort of existence, barely thinking. What is kind appears to be the absence of mind.

Life has been subject to a profound overturning. Before the fall, there was never enough time to do everything I wanted. After, I can never do enough to fill the time.

Doctor II: Happy

"I've had it for seven years," she says, her voice quiet and composed, economizing on energy. "It started when I was thirty-two." She had been a student in my first quarter graduate seminar on Third World writing. At the time, I was told she was ill but gave it little thought. I had not heard of CFS—and she had looked well. Now we've arranged to meet at a pancake restaurant where we're slumping in symmetry across from each other in a booth. Then she tells me about the doctor she's found, a doctor who understands chronic fatigue syndrome and knows how to treat it, though she is so far uncured. "He's so upbeat!" she says. I thank her for her kindness and we make our respective slo-mo exits, as if we are our own species.

When the upbeat new doctor reads Grumpy's paperwork, he says, "Epstein-Barr virus? Oh, no one believes that causes chronic fatigue syndrome anymore. I've got a high antibody count myself." His self is in its thirties and conspicuously fit. "Actually we don't even use that name anymore. We call it 'siffids' now—CFIDS—chronic fatigue immune dysfunction syndrome. It's an immune system illness."

But the odd thing is that Grumpy is right in spite of being wrong. After questions and examinations, Happy concedes with: "I'd say you've got it. Yes, almost definitely." He prods, probes. "Yup, the swollen lymph glands, everything. Officially, in America, we can't call it CFIDS until you've had it for six months—the 'chronic' thing—but you've got it all right. All the symptoms, right down the line. Sudden Onset. Classic." I feel absurdly gratified to hear this.

Over time I learn I am unusual among sufferers in receiving a correct diagnosis from the first doctor I visit. Usually patients—who are most often women—are first told by doctors that they are neurotic and deluded.

"Don't worry," says Happy, "there's plenty we can do." I experience a moment of sweet relief followed by a moment of anger against the other doctor's incompetence, which would have sentenced a less persistent person to a lifetime of untreated illness. We're sitting knee to knee now, his khakis up against my jeans. He's been on the course where they teach young doctors not to put a desk between themselves and the patients. He's full of life, leaning forward, using my first name and insisting I use his, interested in everything I've ever done. We joke; we start off on conversations that we have no time to complete; we are immediately friends.

He's on my side and clearly an excellent advertisement for health and affluence. Outside the suburban house which he has converted into a wellness practice, a Subaru stands ready for the weekend, surfboards strapped to its roof. All this, two kids and a foxy wife too, judging by the photos.

He explains the theory. "That fever that you had before you collapsed? We don't know exactly what it was and it probably doesn't matter. But it left you with a malfunctioning immune system. Somehow it couldn't cope, and has been spinning its wheels. That means you are prey to all sorts of other infections which cause all sorts of physical disregulation. We can deal with some of the symptoms but we can't cure the cause directly, so what we're going to do is build up your immune system so it can fight for us. We remove any causes of immune stress, and give it the nutrients it needs for renewal. The bad news is that this is all new medicine, so unfortunately it will not be covered by your insurance. It's not fair, but that's the price of being cutting edge. OK?"

"OK."

It *is* reasonable.

"We'll give you all the usual tests, of course. Your insurance will pay for those. Come on, I want to introduce you to Heather."

When I fail to spring out of my chair as he has sprung from his, he makes a U-turn at the door to collect me. "Sorry, I was so eager to get you started I forgot you were ill."

Happy leads me through the maze of the house—a humming practice with something going on in every room—until we reach Heather's windowless laboratory in the back.

To Heather, he says: "I want you to meet my friend, writer, professor, world traveler . . . everything. You'll have lots to talk about."

To me: "Heather's a wiz on the Vega machine. We're going to find out which foods stress your immune system. Then we'll give you a diet and supplement it according to your blood test results. Sorry, but this is one test your insurance won't pay for."

To Heather: "Pass my friend on to Majka when you're done, so she can work up the blood tests."

To me: "Make sure you drop by my office before you leave, to say good-bye." And he gives me a slap on the shoulder.

Heather's machine looked like an ancient radio. A pale, shy woman without a white coat, she laughs politely when I ask if it will tell my fortune, and gives me an electrode to hold. She puts test tubes in the machine, spins dials, records results, then changes the tubes. Each one contains a weak dilution of a food, Heather explains. "If the food stresses you, it changes your electrical resistance and the machine detects it. See, your body doesn't like wheat."

When we are done, my diet is down to chicken, rice and a few selected vegetables. The tomato family is out: tomatoes, potatoes, peppers and eggplant. Wheat and maize are out. Anything fungal is out, as is anything made with microorganisms: cheese, bread, most yogurts, vinegar, soy sauce. Fruits and fruit juices are out because they ferment on their own. Sugar because it feeds yeasts in the gut. No alcohol of course. No coffee or tea, except some herbals. And I need to stay away from red meat because of my suddenly elevated cholesterol, which may be my body's response to injury. I can have oatmeal for breakfast if I want, but without sugar, milk, or raisins. Some fish are OK, and too bad for me if I don't like them. On the other hand, I will now be consuming a smorgasbord of nutritional supplements from bottles, kick-starting the new program to transfer my life savings to the manufacturers of alternative medicines.

But all this seems good, the more inconvenient the better, any expense worth it. Strong stuff. I'm taking CFS in hand.

Majka, a cheerful young technician with Spokane's official back-combed hairdo, takes my blood. On her tag, her name is Spokanized to "Miker," to help customers with the difficulty of the foreign. Her underwear shows through the translucent white coat, obvious and innocent. When she's finished, she puts a Donald Duck band-aid on me, pats my arm jauntily, and singsongs, "All done!"

When I go to say good-bye to Dr. Happy, he is wearing a futuristic skullcap from which wires sprout. Heather is hooking it up. "The replacement for the Vega," he explains. "Just giving it a test drive. It measures the electrical activity of the brain directly. Excuse me if I don't get up. Ask Mary-Ellen at reception to make an appointment for the week after next. If she says I'm busy, tell her you're a friend and I insist. Look forward to seeing you." To Heather: "Beam me up, Heather."

List of Names (incomplete)

Chronic fatigue syndrome (current)	America. Hated name.
Chronic fatigue immune dysfunction syndrome	Like CFS, but with attitude.
Myalgic encephalomyelitis, ME disease (current)	Everywhere but America.
Myalgic encephalopathy	The new, improved ME.
Autonomic nervous system dysfunction	New angle.
Hysteria (1997)	Nutty professor.
Postural orthostatic tachycardia dysfunction	You can't stand up.
Gulf War syndrome (1990s)	Wars are bad for you.
Multiple chemical sensitivity syndrome (1990s)	Body can't cope anymore.
Epstein-Barr virus syndrome (1980s)	Made sense at the time.

Chronic mononucleosis	What the E-B virus causes.
Depression (1980s)	Some psychiatrists like this.
Yuppie flu (1980s)	Cruel. *Wall Street Journal.*
Yuppie plague (1980s)	City chicks can't hack it.
Postviral syndrome (1980s)	British. Still makes sense.
Royal Free disease (1970s)	After a British hospital.
La spasmophilie	France.
Tapanui flu	New Zealand.
Low natural killer cell disease	Japan.
Da Costa's syndrome	Holland.
Iceland disease	There too.
Neuromyasthenia	Weak nerves and muscles.
Atypical poliomyelitis	Some connection with polio.
Atypical multiple sclerosis	Some connection with MS.
Fibromyalgia (1960s–)	Painful muscles and joints.
Hypoglycemia (1960s)	Body pulls plug.
Lymphocytic meningo-encephalitis with myalgia and rash	Longest name.
Chronic brucellosis (1950s)	Like in cows, but for longer.

Neurocardiogenic asthenia (1930s)	Heartbeat on the blink
Raggedy Ann syndrome	’nuff said.
Battle fatigue (World War I)	Men.
Effort syndrome (World War I)	Men.
Neurasthenia (nineteenth century)	Victorians take to their beds.
Febricula (early nineteenth century)	A mystery.
The vapors (seventeenth century)	Weak, weak women.

And so on.

I have an illness with many names.
Many names means no name.
An illness with no name may not exist.
Or may be many illnesses.
Or one illness with many forms.
It’s not clear.
A government committee is working on it.

Army III: Marianne

Marianne is a vice president of Inland University and it is from her that I learn most about the place I've come to.

We meet first at an official dinner, after she's made her witty after-dinner speech, just two weeks before I collapse in the gym. I notice the wit, the poise, the fearless public speaking, the smile, the décolletage.

Like Krissy, she had an earlier life in the army. She was the wife of an enlisted man. Hard to imagine that now, her on the edge of fifty, with all that style and gloss. She has short blond hair, and a look that would be at home in Paris.

She comes from somewhere in the middle of America, a farm town where Germans settled and did well, then badly. Marriage was three quick children and big army bases strung across the South, where there was not much else. "A living death," she says, of the life as a noncommissioned wife.

There was a spell on a base in Turkey too, but she never got to know a Turk. She was uppity for the wife of an enlisted man, and the men above her husband warned him to keep her in line, which he took as an order to hit her. She took the kids and left.

Now every time the master sergeant comes to town, the tires of her sports coupe are slashed. She loves her car but never calls the police, just buys new tires. She doesn't want any more trouble with the ex-husband. "That's what he knows to do," she says, "destroy things."

Marianne's talk unwinds with long stories full of her clever charm, and I listen at first because I am enchanted both by this and by the movement of her lips, which I focus on like a French film director. Later, I listen because I am, by now, only capable of listening. I'm drawn to this unexpectedly fascinating woman, unexpectedly encountered in Spokane. She's not—I tell myself—what I am looking for in my soon-to-be-resumed new life in America, an older woman with grown-up children, but I enjoy her company more than anyone else I've met.

It's about twice a year that her ex-husband comes to town to slash her tires. She's a little afraid that sometime it could be her and not her tires, but Marianne has strong nerves.

There are other reasons to be afraid of men. She's the only senior woman at Inland University, and is resented by the old boy cronies who run the place. An ex-lover on the board pushed her into the vice president job, and she's stayed in there, fighting. They want her out and there have been physical threats. She reports to me on the details of the skirmishes. The administrators are corrupt. The campus police chief has plenty on them and calls the shots. The president has recently been arrested for looking up girls' skirts at the Spokane Skymall. He'll get off, she predicts; friends in the city. There was a suspicious death, she confides, but she's got no proof. This is nothing like any university I've known or imagined.

I can, with Marianne, simultaneously be a passive listener and worm my way into the life of the university and Spokane. She's in there and fighting. They've cut the funding for her Women's Crisis Center and given the money to the football team. But she's not giving up. Something in her embraces this combat and she's funny about it, entertaining me. I listen, follow her lips, stroke her hand,

and try not to get too worked up on her behalf against the injustice. She's not without relish at the havoc she sows among the dumb-ox men.

I meet the head of the university once and think him more like a janitor than my idea of a senior academic. No tired, wise eyes, or rumpled distinction. His belt buckle is large and bent downward below his gut. A heavy bunch of keys jangles from his belt. His face gives nothing away. Poker players, not thinkers, are his models.

"You know," I say to Marianne, "I came here with this old-fashioned idea that universities were about learning and the freedom of ideas, not football teams," which makes her laugh.
"Not here," she says. "The alumni want a football team for their money. They get their ideas in church."

"And what about you?" she asks, apropos of her violent husband and the present threats to her safety. "Hasn't there been any violence in your life?" I tell her my family was gentle, with no abuse in it. Then I recount a few glamorous stories from distant places: how the bullets flew in Zimbabwe; how I was threatened with death by evil spirits in The Gambia; how the bombs went off on the North-West Frontier of Pakistan.

Then I find myself telling Marianne, with an intensity that defies the careful husbandry of my energy, about how I was assaulted three times in London in the years before I left. The first time it was by the police after I intervened in their racist attack on a young Nigerian. It's a story that could be presented as heroic and triumphant—an elaborate police conspiracy was uncovered in court—but which I experienced as complicated and disturbing. At the time I had kept it all from my timid, ailing father, who believed so fervently in the goodness of authority. Ours was not a bold family. It was ironic, I tell her lightly, that between my court appearances, I was mugged by a gang of black kids.

Then, most reluctantly, at Marianne's pressing, I arrive at the third assault, a beating I took outside my London home from two men who did not like the way I'd parked my car, and how the London police, now holding a grudge, offered more threat than protection. I forget Marianne is present as I tell how this last event and the public humiliation of it had crushed me and sent me to a darkened room. It had made me thirteen again, the bullied schoolboy. All the confidence of my adult life, I tell her—though up to now I've never told another soul—all the effort, counted for nothing. "It's one reason I left," I admit, only now realizing this to be true. "It wasn't just the difficulties with love, or the opportunity for a new career, it was also that I was certain that it would take too long to rebuild myself in London. I thought I'd do better somewhere new, among strangers."

When I finish, Marianne, steeped in her Women's Crisis Center, thinks for a moment, then says, "It's just the same as when a woman's raped. You were traumatized. You carry the shame in you. Just like I carry the time with the master sergeant in me."

To get me out of the cabin, she drives me up to Canada, two hours to the north, all generosity, me reclined in the passenger seat, her driving swiftly in her fast car, over bumpy country roads, passing pickups with gun racks and backwoods men in them, and all the time talking, joking, talking, me listening.

Then abruptly, she's had enough of fighting the university men. She wants to leave Spokane, and fast. She's had offers. Just turned fifty, gorgeous, poised, a meteoric rise behind her, a growing reputation as a public speaker, activist, and mentor of younger women, the children done with, she's ripe for a move, and is wanted. There's a college in Massachusetts courting her, and a big political job in Washington, DC, hers for the asking, which, when she asks my opinion, I say seems just right for her.

So I'm taken aback when, against my advice to reach out for the East Coast, or an international career beyond, Marianne chooses instead another second-rate university in the middle of America, and within weeks of her arrival is engaged in a war again with the men in power there.

It's four months since my collapse in the gym and the two people I've known best in Spokane, Krissy and Marianne, have both left. I've helped them on their way. I feel like my cabin is a departure lounge for those assembling the courage to leave. When they're here, they are already on foreign land, already half gone. In the greater loneliness I've helped to facilitate, I am newly bereft. On the radio the news is of the war and its brilliant victory. Few American soldiers have been killed. Gulf War syndrome is as yet unimagined. But it's the pervasiveness of the military in ordinary lives that has caught my attention, the secondary, accidental damage of its violence within my friends. We are so far from any enemies here in the Inland Empire that there seems no call for it.

Reasons

I am looking for reasons. This is my culture: sensible, secular, scientific. I possess the reflexive refusal to accept what is given, and a deep belief in the natural dominion of mind over circumstance. That native human willfulness. My mind has set itself upon this course. If cause can be established, remedies might be deduced and control of my existence reasserted. So, I make notes on my symptoms and observe the environment, the weather and the conditions of my life.

For example, the pine trees above the cabin poured a yellow carpet of pollen on me about the time of my first collapse. That might be significant. Possibly, I am suffering from a massive allergy attack.

Then, the seasons were on the turn too, the first hot weather. That might be key.

And I am living downwind of the filthy Hanford Nuclear Reservation where atomic bombs are manufactured. Radioactivity in the air could have sparked something.

Or deer ticks. I've lain out on the riverbank behind the cabin with the deer around me.

Or it could be insecticides from the surrounding farms, which recently were sprayed for the new season.

I notice a book advertised which apparently argues that chronic fatigue syndrome is a variant of AIDS, and that this truth has been suppressed by an official conspiracy. I am not impressed enough by this idea to buy the book, but I have had myself tested. Twice. A part of me is disappointed when the tests come back negative. Part of me wants explanation more than anything.

I have the resources, I argue, to work this out. The education, the intelligence, the confidence. But my mind is finding itself in a difficult tussle, since the more it insists on mastery by mental effort, the more my brain becomes incapable of yielding clear thought. My instinctive solution to the problem of illness makes me ill.

Food is low. I've blown the shopping trip. Yesterday morning seemed like a good time for it. I'd managed some sleep and felt, once again, on the road to recovery. I think my first mistake was to take too many nutritional supplements early in the morning; the resulting nausea was taxing. Then, when I was forced to park a hundred yards away from the supermarket, I should just have given up. Still, I already had a pretty good haul in the cart when it all went wrong. Perhaps I should have tried for less. The eyes, the legs, the brain, all went soft and useless, and I had to face the staring faces as I abandoned the cart in the checkout line and stumbled for the exit, and the safe haven of my pickup's bench seat. Supermarkets, once routine, are proving to be devastating: all those lights, the myriad demands for attention, the refocusing of the eyes, the repeated need for decisions, the walking. I've become a frequent abandoner of supermarket carts.

It's a new day and I'm better again. It's the rain, I decide, that is making me feel better, with its coolness and the way it settles the pollen. All the weights on me have lightened. Or it might have been that meaty stew I ate last night against the current doctor's orders. Maybe I should eat more heartily with less concern for the advice on nutrition. I've lost twenty pounds in two months. My body has never looked better. The fat has burned up, but the muscle is not yet wasted.

On the other hand, I now recall that the last time it rained, I deteriorated, and big meals have not always helped. Sometimes the effort of digestion is itself debilitating. Perhaps this time, it was instead Krissy's visit that set me up, relieving the burden of solitude, and soothing the feeling of lost love.

Or perhaps, contrary to my intuition, this illness is purely psychological after all, a sort of heartbreak. Funny, isn't it, how, since my collapse, I've ached so much over the loss of a young woman I barely knew? She arrived, went back to New York, then returned to Spokane and, finding me newly helpless, hurried away again, this time for good. She could not bear it. The future I had imagined went with her, and the recollection of all earlier losses has poured into the vacated space. She had been the future that held the past in check. I dwell on the love I left behind in England, my old home, my old neighborhood, old friends, old attachments spread across the world. I'm just here now. Stuck.

Come to think of it, when Krissy visited me before, I was not energized by her, but exhausted.

I feel like a blind man stumbling across strange terrain. I walk, fall down, then stand up and continue on, then blunder into marshes and struggle there for weeks, then find myself on airy upland paths, only to plunge over some unimagined precipice, to lie stunned. Then I push myself upright again, always looking for a pattern but always failing to find one. Cause and effect have become disconcertingly unconnected.

There are words for all this, I learn. The bloated, waterlogged discomfort of my brain is commonplace enough among CFS sufferers to have a commonplace name: brain fog. The failure of memory—the names of the people I know best, my telephone number, the name of this town—is typical too, as is my inability to make decisions: "Cognitive dysfunction," I read, and also, "the inability to manufacture new memories." Today, I know the mundane expression of these symptoms through my inability to recall Krissy's name when she arrives, and by my failure, after reading the summary of my medical insurance coverage ten times, to find any of it familiar on the eleventh.

Chronic fatigue syndrome is dissolving my deeply assumed distinction between mind and body, an old understanding of myself falling victim to chemistry. Descartes's assertion that "I think, therefore I am" is challenged daily by the reality that even when I cannot think, I continue, painfully, to be. My mind has become unfamiliar. The brain, somehow aware of its inability to make sense, is alarmed, and a deep, animal portion of the nervous system seizes control, maintaining a state of hyperalertness. It refuses to honor decisions, returning them repeatedly for reconsideration. It forbids the defenselessness of sleep or, if sleep is achieved, the unregulated freedom of dreams. I find the term for this too in the list of symptoms. "Absence of Rapid Eye Movement Sleep," it says.

Danger! Health Care

You need to be healthy to do this. And of sound mind. It is my new job, and is entirely strange to me.

First pile up your bits of paper. On the floor by the couch are the folded sheaves you stuffed into your briefcase each time you left a doctor's office, hospital, or laboratory, usually stamped with a receptionist's smile. Next to them are the receipts you stuffed into your back pocket. In the crack of the cushions are the claims forms you filled out for the insurance company, and the computer-generated screeds of coded benefits paid and denied they have sent to you in return. Resting on your chest, along with the rotary dial phone, are the correspondence and telephone records of your disputes with insurers and providers, including a confusion of scribbled extension numbers and benefit service representative names. It's a day's work to get this far.

You're not used to any of this, the labor of being sick in America. In Britain there had been no paperwork, no dealing with money, no maze. In your youth the government had rewarded doctors simply, like shepherds, according to the number in their flock. You remember visits to the doctor as blithe affairs. The burden of management customary to Americans strikes you as astonishing—staggering—in its complexity, trickery, and venality. You wonder that such a situation could ever be taken as normal.

You are learning the language. There are deductibles and copayments and preapprovals, and other special arrangements that mean the insurance will pay you less than you expect. Sometimes they refuse to pay for particular doctors, sometimes particular treatment from doctors they would otherwise pay for. You are beginning to grasp some of these concepts. They are very annoying. Being annoyed is bad for your health.

Then there are the bills. The monthly insurance company bill. Bills from various laboratories favored by various doctors or insurers for various tests—some of which involved FedExing your feces, urine, or sputum to laboratories in distant states. Bills from hospitals and subcontracting hospital radiologists, mail order pharmacies and, of course, doctors, some of whom will claim the insurance for you, some of whom will not; some of whom will deal with insurance companies, but it turns out not yours. Preferred provider, premier providers, out-of-network providers, providers who require the permission of other providers, all of whom assert that full payment is in the first and final instance due to them from you, the patient.

Sometimes the insurance company refuses to pay because you did not ask them in advance, because you did not know in advance that you had to.

You need an exceptionally good day to tackle this. Several really. Each good day managing health care requires several sick days to recover. The health care is bad for your health.

We won't even talk about alternative practitioners. It's cash or nothing for them.

Once, just after I arrived in Spokane, and before I imagined that I would ever need health care in America, I sat in a parking lot mesmerized by an item on National Public Radio. A personable representative of the health insurance industry was arguing that excluding potentially sick people from health insurance coverage was simply rational business practice, like not insuring bad drivers. The right should be protected from government interference. Sitting there, I was stunned, then angered, by this completely new and savage concept, argued without shame, that a human's blameless need for care was itself a reason for care to be refused. There seemed to be something awful, unacceptable, un-Christian about a place where such a view could be calmly expounded. For a time I feared that I had set about a new life in an entirely wrong place.

OK, you're ready to begin. Before you write any checks you must make calls. There are rules that need interpretation, and interpretations that need negotiation. Nothing is fixed. Since you know your brain is not working well, it's particularly important that you make sure no one is cheating you.

You have quick successes. A payment that has been refused will now be allowed because a customer care representative simply changes the computer code for the treatment. Next, you argue with a laboratory that the amount charged for a self-paid treatment should not be double the amount that the insurance company would have paid if it would in fact pay. They concede, as if they knew they were cheating all along.

Then there are the errors. There are many errors, but it takes work to find them. They are not in your favor. Once found it takes work to correct them. Then more work to repeatedly remind those responsible that the error was corrected and that this should be transmitted to the computer. You rarely speak to the same representative twice, even though you have learned to take their names, and when they give their first names to ask for the family name, though they often puzzlingly refuse this information, as if fearing violent retribution.

This will all be done through free phone lines which insurance companies and billing departments keep understaffed. You must first be on hold for a very long time. Even being on hold is an achievement since it first requires evasion of the automated system. A rotary phone can be an advantage here. After successfully being transferred, you will be put on hold again. Or asked to call back. You must not become exasperated because your brain will fog and ache and fail. One call may take a day.

But in fact you will not do any more of this today. You have done enough. You must go from the couch to bed, postponing until tomorrow—or some other day—the couch with its foliage of papers.

It's a ramshackle affair, this private health care, with its vast quantities of paper and thousands of low-level employees shuffling, sifting, and yet still dumping an unpriced load of office work onto the sick. Apparently, this is what the market can do. You've heard the politician's empty bray, against all evidence, that America has the best health care in the world, that those other systems are bureaucratic, inefficient, socialist.

Army IV: Carol

In the weeks after Marianne leaves Spokane, my only human contact is with Wayne, the landlord. But now and again Carol, my former teaching assistant, calls to ask me how I am. In turn, I ask her about her career plans.

Carol was the best student in my graduate literature class. A single mother in her midtwenties, glasses and fussy clothes. Nothing to notify me.

She had come to my office during my first quarter, rested her elbows on my desk, and after a minimum of flirting, said, "D'you want to fuck?" then smiled sweetly. Her cheeks were dimpled. This was a fantasy realized with striking economy.

I leaned back in my chair, smiled, and banged my head against the wall. "I don't think," I said, "that that would be appropriate," then saw her embarrassed, which seemed a shame for someone delivering a fantasy so efficiently. I added, "Not that I wouldn't like to, of course."
"Don't worry," she said. "I know how to have an affair with a professor." Then she explained that she had known there was something going on between us since our eyes first met in class, finishing with, "You felt it too, didn't you?" In reply to which, I said that I would not like to say, which is the truth, because I had noticed nothing. Though I now looked more closely and saw that

beneath the glasses and the fusty dress, she is pretty and shapely, if not my type.

During my year of teaching, Carol progressed from brilliant graduate student into a trusted teaching assistant, who I depended on to get me through the year. Now she calls me again, to find out how I'm doing.

I am no longer connected to the university, and five months into my illness, I am desperate for company. Why should I push Carol away? She's the only one from the university who remembers me at all.

After she arrives and is lying down next to me, there is yet another army story. A Vietnam vet did it. Mad guy. Fifteen, she was, when he raped her, sixteen when she had his child, twenty-six now.

In her hometown, she says, there were no consequences for the deranged veteran who raped her. He had the local sympathy. It's three o'clock in the afternoon, time passing on a hot day. Outside there is no traffic; the city has left for the mountains and the lakes. I give the matter of effort thought, then raise my arm to put around her. The pressure of her body next to mine is so welcome that I sigh. She's not what I had in mind when I flew in to Spokane, but I'm grateful.

She says, "It's a logging town," and I can picture it, one of those small, bitter places in eastern Washington. The logging industry is struggling and they blame all the world for their troubles. Spotted owls, according to the bumper stickers, made good dinners, and the environmentalists who protect them make good prey. Judging from the stickers, there is a widespread faith in guns as the way to make things right.

"My dad," she says, "thought providing for the family was filling the freezer with deer meat once a year, and he left it at that. Hit my mom. Hit me. He's dead now. He blamed me more than the guy who raped me. They wouldn't turn in a vet. They felt sorry for him." She misses a beat. "Actually, I do too."

She's tells me she has taken her ten-year-old to meet the vet, just so he knows he has a father. She didn't bring up the rape.

She came to Spokane and the university with straight A's, a child, and no money. "I can always get good grades," she says, as if this is a trick that counts for nothing. She'd earned A's from me too, brilliant enough with her literary theory to sometimes overshadow me in class, for which achievement I adored her less than she imagines.

Now I pull her closer, wanting to protect or comfort her, but she doesn't want this soft touch and pulls away.

"I put myself through school," she says, reaching down for me—I'm lying motionless on my back in my accustomed way—"as a prostitute. Are you shocked?" I do not move or speak. "Not the street corner kind. I'd go to the hotels in Spokane and sit there, all demure. When someone wanted to take me home, I'd say I'd love to, but I need some help with money—to cover my nursing shift at the hospital, or for a babysitter, some story. I only went with the ones I more or less liked. Not so different from the girls who did it just for fun. In the end all the hotels banned me, but I had my degree by then."

I hear all this deep inside my spongy brain, where information is unevenly received and not much measured for significance. I am limp in spite of her touch, my whole body limp.
"Sorry," I say, "you probably want to make love."
"You've no idea," she replies, and grins. "But it's OK." She thinks for a moment, then, "I'll tell you about a peak sexual experience."

She met this guy in a bar. Not one of the nice bars, but a rough one outside of Coeur d'Alene. She wasn't working it, she was just there. "He was a lowlife. Lowlifes are attracted to me. Somehow they know where I come from. They see right through the university degrees back to the logging town. Hopeless guys, into guns, petty crime and dealing drugs. They always get caught. Losers. He was good looking, though. A good talker. Are you awake?"

I'm awake, but trying for complete passivity, letting everything slow—breathing, heartbeat, mental activity—so that whatever is in critically short supply in me will not be further expended.

"So, we left the bar and he drove me somewhere, some sort of barn. Tied me from the beams by my wrists. I let him. Then he tore my clothes off me, ripped them, though he didn't have to. He pushed me around like a punching bag at first, then he fucked me. Both ways. You know, up my ass too. Drove me crazy. Then he came all over me. After that, he fixed his clothes without saying a word, but before he left, he peed all the beer he'd drunk, hosed me down from top to bottom. It felt so dirty. It was," she whispers in my ear, "the best!"

When I ask what happened next, she dismisses the question with, "Oh, we met up a few weeks later, had a talk, made friends, sort of. You can only do that with someone once." Then, reaching down again, "Excuse me, Professor, but I'm going to fuck you now."

But, Carol is leaving Spokane too. She's not doing the doctorate she's capable of, or even traveling far. She's never left the state, never been on a plane. She's going for teacher's training in another Inland Empire town. "More practical," she says, dismissing other possibilities. I keep telling her she's brilliant and could go far. "What's the point?" she asks, exasperated.

I last see her at the bus stop. She's insisted that I should not make the effort to drive her home, and I've readily conceded. I'm wrecked and ruined, used and grateful. It's hard to imagine a bus will ever come along. I can't remember when I last saw one. The debris where she stands is undisturbed by other feet. She waits, smiling, seemingly delighted with herself. Above her there is a sad bus stop sign on its pole, America's little loser's flag. "Don't worry," she says, "I'm fine."

Quietness

The quietness is complete now. And with this solitude grows a low-grade, persistent panic. All those I met while I was well have now left Spokane. The social capital of my healthy life is fully spent. This is my new American life: not much. It's October and it's taken me a year to go from everything being possible to nothing being possible.

On the plane above Spokane, I had wondered who I would meet down here, who might stick. None has. Instead, the women I've met and cared about have been less settled than me, more troubled, more eager to move on. Rather than embarking on a new, vigorous life, I've listened passively to the lives of others. Their fading voices are in me, telling of intimate hurts, the incidental violent overflow of military life carried in them. By association it's mine too now. Spokane's sweet young men and women reservists are on the TV news again, returning from war to pick up the babies they put down to fight, alive but something new in them now.

I receive a letter from a yacht broker in England. My boat has been sold. So, I'm OK. I'd forgotten about the boat. A year ago I was making plans to sail it to America, a great adventure. I'd arrive in New York and live on the boat there, close to the artist girl. I understand that I am no longer that person.

From the window of the cabin, I can see a distant road bridge, where the RVs of the elderly are crawling south for winter. The people of Spokane are on the move too, returning from their summer places, the pickups towing boats, horse boxes, all-terrain motor toys, summer clutter, even golf carts. I wonder whether I will still be here to see the pickups take up their winter tasks of plowing snow and carrying snowmobiles. I cannot conceive of how I could still be here, or how I could not.

Out of necessity, I take the illness for my company, something with its own intelligence. It has its personality and I have mine. As I try to train it, it sets about training me. If I walk too far or fast, it punishes me. If I attempt work, it makes my nervous system buzz and fizz with flaring short circuits. It wants me quiet and it wants me flat, and I would do well to obey. It wants slowness and routine. Excitement and ambition anger it. It is appalled by spontaneity, hates decisions, refuses responsibility. It tells me to be quiet and satisfied, has no truck with upset. I take it with me to doctors and ask to be rid of it.

My decisions are routinely returned to me, by the governing mental regulator which informs me that my calculations are all unreliable. Also, that I should never forget that I am deciding for two. We are at odds. I want from America what new arrivals want: an accelerated life, making homes, money, reputation, family. What CFS wants is a minimal sufficiency, a place to lie down among kindly people. We are in a three-legged race, each hobbling the other. Sometimes I seem to be making progress, then CFS exercises a casual sovereignty.

The cabin is no place for us. Winter is approaching and there are no friends left. I think we might do better in London where I know people, and I set about booking a ticket.

There are the usual complications of comparing the prices of different airlines according to availability, dates and routes. To this I add new computations, involving the distance to be walked at various airports where I might change planes, and the waiting time between flights, both limited by my abilities, which are impossible to calculate. I put tickets on hold and then fail to confirm them within the requisite twenty-four hours, then try again, introducing into the calculation new knowledge of the declining number of available seats revealed to me by various airline agents. Unable to decide, I successfully persuade one airline representative in Missouri, who is possibly—I discover later—a subcontracted prison inmate, to hold the reservation for an additional two hours to allow for the later midnight in my time zone, but by the time this period has also elapsed I'm aflame with dysfunction, my brain reduced to emergency alarms forbidding the transaction of any business. I let the booking lapse, and the failed effort is such that days pass before I can again assemble the wherewithal to make any new plan.

There are words for these symptoms too: dyscalculia, sequencing dysfunction, abstract reasoning dysfunction, and so on. I don't know this yet, so it seems like it's just me.

In any case, England is no solution. I cannot physically or organizationally pack up my life, and a premature return is deeply repellent. I came to America to make a new life. I'm not ready to fail. I will be well soon.

I consider where else I might go for the interim. I have a friend in New Mexico, one in Montana, and one in Massachusetts. I do not know the one in Montana well enough. The one in Massachusetts is in no shape to help. The New Mexico one lives in a quiet mountain village where, a few years ago, I spent the winter looking after his farm. An old place in America. That feels like it could be the seed of a life.

The friend finds a house for me to rent in the village, which I first accept, then reject when I understand I will have to furnish it, an impossible task. Then a neighbor of my friend, an acquaintance I made on my earlier visit, steps forward to offer me a room in her house, now that her daughter has left for college. Ready furnished and welcoming, it settles in my mind as my best—my only—bet.

October is bringing the first hint of winter cold to Spokane. There is nothing here for me.

To seal the decision, my twenty-four-year-old nephew is taken with the idea of a road trip down the spine of the Rockies, and generously offers to come to Spokane, load my pickup, and drive me out of there, south to New Mexico. We leave in early November, just ahead of the snows.

New Mexico, 1991–1994

Settlers I

The roads are dirt and the houses are made from earth. Most of the inhabitants customarily speak Spanish. Their tiny farms are irrigated by hand-dug ditches that lead water away from the valley's central river and release it into fields by means of simple wooden gates. It's a peasant society in all its lineaments, except that many of the farms are neglected and the farmers often have menial jobs thirty-five miles away at the Los Alamos National Laboratory.

Invitations from my earlier career still find me. Various UN agencies have invited me to visit Indonesia, Pakistan, Fiji and Uganda, to address the problems of their rural poor. Because I expect to recover soon, and will want to earn some money, I do not discourage them. I say I am busy, and let them imagine that I am in great demand and hard to get.

I can see much of the shape of this village by tottering fifty yards up the garden of this house to where there is first the humped bank of an irrigation ditch, then an eroding cliff face leading up to the high mesa. Going twenty yards in the other direction, I'm at the river, slow this time of year, and its bosque of red willows, which love the water and make a ribbon between the river and the fields.

But most of my time is spent lying down on a new couch, held still by the weight in me. It's not the worn, tweedy, soft couch that came with the Spokane cabin, but an austere wooden couch in

Santa Fe style, softened, but not much softened, by cushions of coarse Native American fabric. I like the flatness that comes with the hardness, but after hours of lying down bits of me go numb. Nor does my body like the remedy, which is to shift onto my side, since it seems that this demands a greater muscular effort. With CFS I am privy to such minute and surprising knowledge.

The reason I am in an ancient peasant village in America is ultimately because Jack and Clara, and their friend, my current landlady, a jewelry maker, moved here from cities, settled, and stayed. They are not Hispanics, but members of the Anglo minority. While the Hispanics have been here since the sixteen hundreds, and the Native Americans before that, the Anglo community dates back to the 1960s and the hippie diaspora. That moment of history coincided with my first spell of living in America. My student perspective registered it as war protests, disaffection with government, reaction against capitalism and consumerism, a wish to create an alternative culture, and the confidence that this could be done. The counterculture. Some came to New Mexico and found this old, cheap, beautiful, overlooked place, and invited themselves in. They started small farms, made arts and crafts, and experimented with communal living, free love and drugs. It was a great, brave project that never impressed the locals, who remain separate and austerely skeptical.

Many of the Anglos stayed for only a short time before burning out, or drifting back to the cities and careers. But some saw the experiment through, survived the excesses, worked hard, raised children, built homes, and achieved most of their dream of a healthy life, safe and simple, and almost completely beyond the notice of government. They had pulled off, or nearly pulled off, that element of the American dream that completely leaves behind the past and replaces it with a fully imagined new life. Inevitably, I am now dreaming of this for myself. I could, as soon as I recover, sell my London flat and buy a little land here, and one of those delightful old adobe houses, farm a little, write a little, live modestly, find a wife, have children, and never return to the mad distraction of movement and achieving that has done me no good. I, too, could be a settler.

During my first days here, before my landlady quits the house in order to pursue a man in Texas, she and Jack kindly invite a good portion of the Anglo community over to meet me. Their friends are mainly couples in their forties, fifties and sixties, mostly well read and educated, mostly struggling to make ends meet as artists in one of the poorest regions of America. They are all kind, and all eager to hear the story of someone new, or to test their wits against him. I struggle to hold conversations and to explain my inability to sit up or talk for too long. I am learning the etiquette of being ill among strangers. I tell them, believing it more or less, that many people with CFS recover in a year or two, and that my present, awkward stage is one of recuperation and recovery. I say it is a foolish illness, not worth taking seriously, and they generally agree. I recognize some of these people from my first, exuberant visit to the village just four years before. They are the early Anglo settlers, the counterculture idealists. Jack says, sadly, that the more recent arrivals rarely share the same energy, but are generally just disappointed men, more refugees than settlers.

How to Be Ill

You know how to be ill.
You are plucky and cheerful
You do not complain
You maintain a genuine interest in the lives and problems of others
Even when these problems are clearly of a lesser order
You laugh at yourself
You overcome your disabilities to shine in spite of them
You have great spirit
You are an inspiration to all and trouble to none
You transcend.

By contrast
Those who do not know how to be ill
Remind others of how they feel
Whine
Become cantankerous
And impose their ill fortune on all around them
Spreading emotions of sympathy, guilt and disgust
You deplore such people.

The ideal sick person is paralyzed
But with a brilliant brain and a big heart
He or she has huge disadvantages
Yet is winning through,
Personality intact.

A clear course toward death is an advantage for the high achieving invalid
The legs are amputated
The end is imminent
The mind blazes with a selfless wisdom.

Sufferers from CFS are not good at being ill.

You look well
You are not dying
Your complaint is modest
You are going to be trouble for a long time
Your brain does not work
Your charm has gone with it
You are inconsistent
Sometimes perversely well.

You are unreliable
You explain your unreliability
Which is like whining
You cannot explain your illness
You are inconvenient, thoughtless, boorish, charmless, witless
And don't do your share
You are not yourself.

There is no place for people who are not themselves
You are not good at being ill.
You will lose all your friends
You may kill yourself because of this.

Home II: Adobe

It's in the old style: mud brick walls a foot thick, viga ceilings, single story, soft edges, painted window frames with the color bleached out by sun. Check out houses like this on the postcards sold in Santa Fe.

Mine is located in a mountain village between Santa Fe, Los Alamos, and Taos. The valley it occupies is shaped like an eye. You enter at the narrow end, through a crack between mesa cliffs, and it flares out into a fertile landscape of tiny fields. At the far end, a mile distant, the valley rises to meet the mesa, drawing itself together into a mountain pass. This house is not in the central village, but on a field caught between the river and the mesa wall. It's perfect, beautiful. I'm living in someone's dream.

There's a tree house at the bottom of the garden, just before the cliff. I once surprise the neighbor's fourteen-year-old daughter there, splayed naked in the sun on its open deck, a teenage boy inside her, right as Eden.

Now that the owner of the dream has run away in pursuit of a late love, I am alone here. It's very quiet. The early days of my novelty have passed and I see little of anyone, a great contrast to my previous visit, when I was healthy, energetic, and a prized social addition. Now I mainly offer helplessness.

The house is not old, but was built thirty years ago by my landlady and her architect ex-husband when they were young. Adobe houses like this are no longer built by the locals, who are neither wealthy, nor inclined to unnecessary manual labor, nor inflamed by retro ideals. The newlyweds among them favor air-conditioned manufactured homes put down on the farmland abandoned by their parents.

The design of the house is the old Hispanic style of the region, but the idea of it has passed through Anglo minds before arriving back here. It addresses a hunger that it was thought might be satisfied by something old and wise belonging to a different place.

In the way they maintain cool in summer, the thick adobe walls are perfect. The roof is constructed of wood and clay, and it leaks in acceptable, ancient ways during heavy rain. This is a dry climate; moisture does not linger. For a floor there is thin cement set directly on the earth and stained red in parts, polished to sometimes yield pink, sometimes gray, as irregular as nature. This should be wonderful. I should be full of joy to be in this wonderful place. But during my entrapped and immobile days here the word that plays in my mind is "sarcophagus."

Outside is just too large. And too hilly. My legs will not take me anywhere beyond the riverbank, where I unsuccessfully try for peace by forgetting myself in nature. But I don't find peace; an agitation for connection and love overwhelms it. I want a life. The nearest town is over twenty miles away, and the effort of driving there to shop is daunting. It's a large landscape and I feel small in it.

I have the nagging sense that in this village I am a rude intruder into a fragile culture belonging to others. The other Anglos seem not to share this scruple but have instead the sense of claiming something undervalued and neglected in their own country, a found object to enjoy and treasure. There's an intimacy to the village and our presence feels to me like entering the living room of strangers and making ourselves at home on their favorite furniture. The resentment should be expected.

In this I can also argue that I am the one against nature. The history of mankind is a history of awkward migrations. This valley experienced waves of Native tribes, then the Spanish, then intermingled tribes and Spanish, including Jews fleeing the Inquisition.

I recognize the irrigation system on which the village's existence has long depended as similar to the ones I've seen in the Hindu Kush of Pakistan. The mud houses in both places are also of a type. I posit a connection: Arab knowledge coming up into Spain and from there migrating west to America—its legacy proved by enduring Arabic terms in the local irrigation terminology—and in the other direction, Arab knowledge spreading east with Islam to Pakistan, bringing the same technology with it. Lying on this long, hard couch—the traditional Hispanic woodwork and Native American upholstery combined by an Anglo carpenter—I stretch out in the extent of the connection.

I imagine the novel I will write when I am able. It will be about human migration and will take me far from here. The Arab-Asian-European-African city of Zanzibar seems like a good starting point, and a woman I met there, who seemed to contain the blood of the whole world in her, could be a promising basis for a character. I'll write from her point of view, and instead of a halted Englishman in America, I'll be a lively, multiracial woman from Zanzibar.

My landlady has encouraged me, in her absence, to use her more comfortable bedroom with its overstuffed bed, curtained canopy, Japanese erotic prints, and the stone bath set directly into the ground. I cannot. This house is too much her dream, and I feel so slight and still now that I fear any surrender to the tastes of another. Instead, I use the barely furnished room that once belonged to her daughter.

Doctor III: Stress

Doctor III, a polished man, too far away in Santa Fe, asserts that he knows nothing of chronic fatigue syndrome, or myalgic encephalomyelitis, or such things. He wears this ignorance with pride, as if it is a specialized approach with which he combats the follies of fashion. He affects bemusement at the diagnosis and talks instead of the deep mysteries of stress, leaning back in his chair to emphasize his own presently evolved state of relaxation. "I had something like that myself," he offers, "during my first year as a doctor. All sorts of odd symptoms."

He's gone silent now, lost in the past, then recovers to ask, "Are you married?"
"No. I was with someone, but we broke up."
"Ah!" he says, vindicated.

There was the stress of love, of course, of loss. And the move between countries. I've heard that moving counts as stress, the loss of the familiar and the abrasion of the strange. So, I suppose I piled it on in a way, with the move, the job, the anxiety about teaching, finishing the novel to deadline—which, as it happens, was about the breakdown of a middle-aged man, a joke that's now on me. In that story I used physical illness to symbolize an inner crisis. Now it seems like a cheap trick.

But the fact is, isn't it, that I've done all this before: new countries, new jobs, heartbreaks, hard work, facing down timidity. It is not stress, but life.

Looking at Doctor III, I think I see what stress is: it's what comes to doctors' lips when their conceit outstrips their understanding.

Now he's offering antidepressants. I can, if I like, have a pile of them, free, off the shelf, off the record, no stigma, just dropped off by the drug rep. He indicates a slew of little boxes. "I don't feel depressed, I feel ill," I tell him. He nods, humoring me: "Stress can present like that." To which I point out that doctors used to say the same about stomach ulcers until they were proved to be caused by a bacterium. "Oh, that," he replies, unruffled. "That story was more complicated."

He's coolly professional now, my minutes up, and ensures himself against his own complacency by expressing a pro forma willingness to order up any number of tests to eliminate the testable. I decline.

The Prize

She says, softly into the silence, not looking at me, Zoe playing across the room, she says, thrilling me, "I think I'm a good mother, but I'm not sure I'm a good wife."

Then Mary lifts her eyes to fix on mine, through the fall of her hair.

Five weeks now since the unexpected knock on the heavy door of the old adobe house. I'd called out, "Yes?" from where I lay on the couch, and when nothing further developed, heaved myself upright to investigate. The knock was shocking in my solitude. It was two months since my landlady left and I'd had no visitors.

Standing outside, the bright light of the day behind her, was a slender, dark-haired woman, tallish and wearing a long skirt, to which clung a small girl. I knew who she was, so in spite of the light's dazzle, I knew she was beautiful. I'd seen her in the village, heard her laughter, been smitten. My landlady, with a bitchy edge, had referred to her as "the prize."

In her low, clear voice, Mary said, at the open door, "We're going shopping in Taos. I heard you were ill and wondered if we could get you anything, whether anyone was doing that for you."
"Thank you," I said. "No, no one is. I'm managing. Please, come in."
"Oh," she said. "By the way, I'm Mary. And this is my daughter, Zoe. I should have mentioned it before." She'd laughed then,

something livelier and more reckless than her voice. But still she advanced only a foot beyond the threshold. For propriety, I thought. Zoe, five then, was unsure about the whole enterprise, holding back and peering past me into the cool, dim house.

"I could use some mineral water," I said. It was vitally important that I request something. "Fizzy. And maybe some Carr's water biscuits?" For reasons I've forgotten, these were then part of a recommended diet and were not available at the village shop.
"Will Perrier do?"
"That's my current favorite."
Mary nodded decisively. "I'll drop them around tomorrow afternoon."

There was nothing about her that could be said to be flirtatious.

Mary was the prize because she was the loveliest Anglo woman in the village, and the most accomplished and admired. Among the wives, she was, at thirty-seven, among the youngest. Further, it was also grudgingly agreed, she was nice. A little self-contained, but nice. She had a good doctorate in paleontology, and some minor national celebrity as an expert on dinosaurs. Her husband, older than her and the village's tallest and most handsome Anglo man, had found her digging up bones in Africa and had brought her back to New Mexico. The prize.

Over five weeks Mary advanced in stages to the kitchen counter, where she deposited the bags of shopping, to brief conversations standing, to conversations sitting, then to staying for afternoon tea, which she revered, like all things English and Victorian. She had grown up in Los Angeles, but appeared untouched by its most famous tendencies, not unduly cheerful, beguiled by wealth, or blond. Early on, I once caught her unawares, alone and happily laughing at her book, which turned out to be—enchantingly for me—Chaucer's *Canterbury Tales*.

In the same five weeks, five-year-old Zoe had advanced from pulling on her mother's skirt to leave, to sitting on her mother's knee to interrupt, to sitting on my knee out of a sense of fairness, to playing happily on her own while leaving us to talk.

Now Mary, who is by nature private, has made a confession and is holding my eye, while I am holding my breath, wondering what this could mean, that she is not a good wife. I want this gentle woman's company so much, and I believe I have no chance of it. In the end, words seem too risky so that I simply nod, to acknowledge that I have heard something and have attached importance.

Doctor V: Anomaly

Knowing no one, knowing no better, I find him in the yellow pages, under Physicians—Urology.

"This is what I do," he says without inflection, his forefinger up my rectum, massaging my prostate to milk some fluid from it. "This is what I do all day, every day."

I'd bled one night, bright blood. "Well, you've either got an acute prostate infection, or cancer," is his calm verdict.

The blood cheers me up. It's the first time I've had such a clear, indisputable and traditional symptom. Though by the time I reach the doctor, weeks later, the brightness has gone, leaving only a dark tint to my urine as evidence.

I like him, a quiet-spoken, gray-bearded man, an Anglo displaced in a poor Hispanic town. Not from around here. He has sad eyes that linger with sincerity, as if there are words he would passionately like to speak, but cannot. There must be a story, and it seems that he might tell it, leaning back in his desk chair regarding me. I mention, by way of conversation, that I have a friend—it is Mary, in fact—who was considering retraining as a doctor. "Tell him not to even consider it," he responds definitely. "It's no life these days. Not with the HMOs. You can't be a good doctor anymore." I do not correct him about the gender.

I like him because he seems sad, and kind. He is never in a hurry to move on to the next patient. About the CFS that rules my body and my days, he is dismissive. He is not even sure he has ever heard the name. I describe the symptoms, the comprehensive oddity of it, and he cuts me short to deny the connectedness of things. "That's nothing to do with this," he says. "It's outside my expertise."

"We'll try antibiotics first, and if they cure it, we'll know it's an infection. If they don't, it's cancer."
"And if it is cancer?"
"If it is cancer, then perhaps you'll die."

His demeanor is relaxed, melancholy. He's not trying to shock me. Rather his tone suggests that death would not be such a bad thing, that it is something we could all embrace and share, that he wouldn't mind a bit of death himself.

I nod thoughtfully, acknowledging that he has given me something to think about. Turning to the window, he says, "That's my truck outside, the one full of rocks. I'm making a garden at my house. That's what I like to do."

I make up a story about him, over the course of months. He's a gay man who has come here from a big city. I imagine for him a gregarious metropolitan life full of intelligence and sex. And I imagine how it might have been for him when his friends started dying from AIDS, him the doctor among them, the doctor who knew about sexually transmitted diseases. He came to rural New Mexico because he could not bear it anymore, his losses, his helplessness. He has become so used to the closeness of love to death, that death seems like a sort of love to him, almost a blessing. I am being invited to join his set.

We develop a slight friendship within the doctor-patient bounds. Once I phone him at his home—he has suggested I visit his garden—but a different, suspicious, annoyed man answers, putting me off. I find that I am reluctant to point out that I am heterosexual in case we lose our rapport, so I say nothing, do not mention Mary. In any case, Mary is absent these days. She left the village two weeks ago and has been entirely silent.

I wonder if my carefulness is a sort of flirting, because I am lonely. I look forward to my office visits, which are marked by a series of antibiotics, each of which fails to remove the symptoms and moves me closer to the proof of cancer. Each treatment leaves me a little weaker.

I give him a copy of the novel I finished in Spokane that has now been published, writing a note of my esteem in it, and he clasps the present in both hands, his eyes misting. The sex in the book is heterosexual and on subsequent visits I think him more reserved.

The last of the antibiotics is a sulfa drug, the oldest, crudest remedy. It drives me deep into illness, rarely able to leave my bed. When finally I am able to return to his office, he does his test.
"No sign of infection, but the blood's still there."
"Which means I have cancer."
"Yes. We need to look inside."

"You talked a lot under anesthetic," he says. "You were like another person. The nurse asked if you were always as lively as that. I said you weren't."
"So, what did you find?"
He looks at his desk, then up at me, trenchant. "I found nothing."
"Nothing?"
"Nothing that shouldn't be there."
"I don't have cancer?"
"You don't have cancer." He is stern, formal, as if concerned that finding me without cancer might be a serious disappointment.
"Then what's causing the blood?"
He shrugs, interest lost. "You have an anomaly."

I feel I have let him down, walking away from death, like a soldier being sent home on the eve of battle.

Waiting for Mary

Mary's visits have stopped without warning. One week, two, three, more. Thoughts of her tick away the endless, useless time. "Call!" I instruct her out loud, "Mary, call me!"

One day I run into her husband outside the post office where we all collect our mail—there is no home delivery down the village's dusty tracks. He has always been friendly and now he asks me about the Santa Fe belly dancer who is my new next door neighbor. "If I was a single man like you . . . ," he says, and laughs. He has striking blue eyes, and is a loud talker who peppers his talk with little challenges to maintain an upper hand.
"Mary's well?" I ask, trying for nonchalance.
He leans back and appraises me before replying: "Last I heard. Off on one of her trips."

Mary has said of her husband: "He's not a bad man. He can't help being overbearing."

Zoe is wafted from the post office by adoring Hispanic women, and is returned to her father at a rush, embracing his legs and asking to be lifted. Collecting a rejection, she unselfconsciously wanders over to hang on my legs instead, causing a puzzled hesitation in her father before he tells her too sharply not to bother me.

The weeks pass with no Mary. Months. I visit the doctor, am given my sentence and my reprieve, and still no Mary. "Call me!"

I cry out aloud to the echoing house. She is my hope. “Mary, call me,” I add more softly.

Luck

It's been a lucky life.

I was born
Just after the last war
Just after the Welfare State
Which fortuitously ensured
The survival of an asthmatic child
From a poor family

My parents stayed married
And loved me
They did not hit me
They did not die young
They did not become destitute
Or require my support
They were always nice to my girlfriends
Whatever the girlfriend's race

I lived in a democratic country
Which became steadily more prosperous
The pleasures increased
The hardships diminished
Class barriers eroded
In time for me to cross them
Government schooling was free
And popular

I went to university when students were paid
And earned a doctorate on full salary
No discomfort
Lucky

Conscription ended
Five years before it was my time
Britain kept out of Vietnam
Which would have been my time.

The pill was widely and quickly adopted
Soon after I first had sex
And miniskirts came in just then
When I was young
Young was the thing to be
I had more sex than my parents
In America
Then in Africa
Before we'd heard of AIDS
And did not suffer guilt
Only the wish for more

I worked in poor countries
When we still believed we could help
Was well paid for it
Bought a flat in England
That doubled in value
Sold it and bought another
Which doubled too
Bought a boat
My timing was right

When I wanted to go to Africa
An offer came out of the blue
When I wanted to go to America
An offer came out of the blue
Lucky

I wrote a novel
Which was immediately published
The language I learned as a child
Was the world's most useful language
I was white, male and Christian
When all of these were winners
Have loved and been loved by
Admirable women.

I traveled the world
And generally found myself
To be well liked
My digestion has been excellent
I have not lost everything in a natural disaster
I have not been tortured for my beliefs
My savings have not disappeared overnight
There have been no unwanted pregnancies
That I know of
My dog has been a very good dog
Lucky

My life has been without terror or deprivation
With as much choice as the world has ever offered
Yet frequently I have been unhappy
And complained
And I must apologize for this.

Skepticism

I've tried to explain my illness to my friend Jack and his wife, Clara. I suspect them of skepticism, and because I admire them it's important to me that they should believe that my illness is physical and not something psychological that I could overcome with moral firmness. They are on my mind for much of the time it is not devoted to wondering about Mary, but I see little of them. Though their house is close by, the terrain requires a circuitous route that is too far to walk, and I am in any case reluctant to impose myself. In an emergency these are the friends I would need to turn to for help, and they are cautious. Their lives are already too full and too arduous.

Jack has hinted at quiet doubts about my illness, as if to give it credence would be to give it power. He is stoic in his own life. Illness is the curse that hangs over them, which could tip their lives into disaster overnight, the unmentionable terror, the inevitable end. They cannot afford health insurance. Instead of security, their return to the soil has given their lives fragility. Their only remedy would be to turn to their families and the old money accumulated in the old ways that they have repudiated. Like poor villagers in Africa and Asia, illness is the bolt from the heavens that they most fear. When I first met Jack, and he told me that they had no health insurance and that an illness or accident could ruin them forever, I was still living in Europe and was horrified to discover educated people in a rich country living with such fear. My concern stirred up the anxiety in him and left him discomposed, irritated. Now I see how a national pitilessness in health care can cause a contagion of personal pitilessness, even among its kindest citizens. Illness makes Jack nervous, and he wants to believe it is a matter of choice. He lives wisely; the sick have themselves to blame.

I give Jack a brochure on CFS aimed at better informing those who know a sufferer. He glances at the heading, then puts it aside and changes the subject. Later, Clara picks it up. When she next talks to me, she says, "I think I have CFS." She is the first of many. She says, "I'm always tired. My memory is terrible. I can't sleep. But I can't just stop working like you."

I quiz Clara on her symptoms, then conclude that her complaint probably is not CFS, which irritates her, as if I unfairly claim a privilege that I deny to her. She is exhausted and discontented, and would like an illness to be the cause.

So, it was with some relief that I first carried the diagnosis of prostate cancer to my friends. It was a better way to be ill, the blood, the cancer, the incurable finality. I was nearly cheerful. Jack was thoughtful, Clara concerned.

Subsequent news of my anomaly is embarrassing. Clara's thrifty store of sympathy had been raided to no purpose. Jack's skepticism is affirmed. I am left with just the old illness—no blood, no death—the illness with the silly name that seems to say that I've just been tired for a while, and may always be.

The Gift of Illness

"God, I've missed you," I say, not meaning to. I hug Mary close, then scoop up Zoe from the doormat.
Mary nods gravely before speaking. Then, "It was necessary for me to do that. To go away."
"But you're back now?"
"Yes," she says, "in a sense," and withdraws her eyes.

She's keeping Zoe close to her, hungry for her daughter. But her touch stays light and her voice is soft with a fastidious respect for a child's autonomy that is outside my own experience. It's a scrupulous, unpossessive love.

On the day Mary first visits alone, after taking tea, the two of us standing by the door, I kiss her, and find a speculative willingness in her lips. I had not been sure. She holds on to me, then lets her arms drop loose where she stands, offering me the run of her.

"I'm lucky," she says, a little later, looking down, a naturalist observing, "I didn't lose my breasts after Zoe."

Enough for today, we agree, without saying it. I carefully re-cover her, an act more intimate than baring.

When we are done, Mary lets go of quietness and laughs, cheered up by the bad behavior.

As she is leaving, she says, "There's a problem with my coming here. The dogs." And she indicates the two disreputable ones waiting for her outside, one yellow, the other gray. "If I walk here, they follow me and let everyone know where I am. Leaving the car outside would be worse."

I've said nothing about a next visit, and think it better to say nothing now, in case it halts this pleasing train.

"I'll manage somehow," she concludes.

Mary arrives on a bicycle, flushed from outdistancing the dogs. "Well," she says, once inside, after we kiss, her breathless animation meeting my surprise, "Are you going to get into my underwear, or what?"

I do not care if the effort floors me for a week. This is not the time to let CFS defeat me, with both its future and mine in the balance. Our interests are congruent for once: my aspirations, its care.

Mary and I undress separately, lie down face to face. Her hands are rough from excavating dinosaurs, so that the tenderness of her touch is edged excitingly with the rasp of practicality. I draw my finger across the pale skin of her stomach, which holds the mark for moments, reddening. Soft, no longer very young. We move closer, into each other.

"Not bad," she says later, "for an invalid."

Dusk has covered us while I lie stunned into blankness by the shocking exertion, my perverse heart thumping slow in response to the requirement that it beat more quickly. It's so slow that each new beat seems to be an event. Mary is standing, smiling, already dressed, and has just kissed me lovingly. I remember that the lovemaking was lengthy, a virtue forced on me by my inability to progress quickly toward climax. She says, "I hope I haven't killed you. You've been out for a while. Don't move. Just lie there." I hold on to her hand so that she adds, "I have to go. He'll be wondering. Zoe too."

On another day, lying next to me, she says, "There's something I have to tell you." I wait. "You know, when I went away . . . I was with someone. I left my husband for someone. He doesn't know. It was a mistake. I needed to tell you. I've been dreading it."

So, while I was here alone calling out for Mary, she had been making love to someone else, planning a life with him. For long moments I think about this, and about how I feel, and what it means, her brilliantly achieved deceit. Not for a second had I guessed. But it is too late for reconsideration. My heart and hopes are all attached. "It's all right," I say.
Her response is too quick. "Thank God," she says. "Now I can start breathing again."

Lovemaking lifts me and flattens me, leaving me helpless as a beached whale. In between Mary's scarce, irregular visits, my mind falls into a troubled, cranky indecisiveness. I am not equal to this affair. I am not equal to Mary, and not equal to her husband. If he was to come noisily to my front door one night, I would not be equal to his fists. I regret that the door cannot be locked. The absence of locks is a matter of pride to my landlady. I am unfit to steal a bold man's wife, not strong enough, not confident enough, unequal to either the role of lover or husbandly provider.

We move quickly to the practicalities; we are both desperate; we need to get out of town. I volunteer that I own a flat in London that I might sell, and that I have a little money saved, and the money from the sale of my boat in England. She says she has a little money too, from when her mother died. We'd be all right for a year or two, maybe three, even if her research funds dry up and I stay ill. Neither eventuality is likely, we each assure the other.

Mary says that now her mother has died, she needs a family more, making the cost of leaving her marriage high for her, and suggesting to me by this that there will be room in her life for me, but that I must never leave her.

I tell Mary that to the world she appeared exceptionally able, exceptionally self-contained, gifted. "You've no idea," she replies. "You've no idea. Inside, I feel tiny, too small for the world. It's my secret. I've never told anyone." I say that I think I understand.

In time, I come to realize that it is the enforced patience and humility of illness, my new gentleness, that has most drawn Mary to me. Her husband's domineering ways had come to offend her for the way they roughed up her quiet deliberations, her secretiveness, her tender self. She believes that what is within her is worthy of defense from a plundering man, and with me she feels safe. In health, I might have tried to match, impress, or capture her, and from this she would have shied away. But, in illness, she is mine.

Doctor VIII: Medicine Lite

A real doctor. But also a homeopath.

She's a nice, cheery woman, short gray hair flopping forward jauntily. Fit. Sexy at sixty. She is delighted to hear of my symptoms. They are apparently terrific symptoms.

"OK," she says, "let's see," and goes to a big book with battered hard covers of a faded blue. "It'll tell me the remedy," she explains. She is completely confident. "OK, here it is!"
This is marvelous. How could I have waited for so long?

No effect.

"OK," she says next time, not discouraged, "there are others. Tell me your dreams."
I have no dreams to tell her. I have no dreams.
"Never mind, this will do it," she assures me, standing, holding a vial of an undetectable dilution in one hand, a finger of the other keeping her place in the big book. She is so confident, so full of life. You can't help liking her.

No effect.

"Oh," she says, still untouched, still keen. "Want to carry on?" As if this is our game.

I'm tending to think she's on something that instills perpetual delight through freedom from any sense of consequence. But she is a real doctor.

"No, not for now," I say, no longer optimistic. "How much do I owe you?"

She has no receptionist, just a room in a quaint old adobe house, downtown in Santa Fe. Her practice gives an airy impression of lightness and grace. That she does not deal with health insurance does not matter, since I'm in a period when I can't find anyone to insure me. "Oh," she says, consulting the ceiling, laughing. "Let's say three hundred."

Not that much for a doctor. I pay. I leave. We've barely met.

Love at Last: Mary

Mary manages everything.

In summer, after I meet Mary, I leave New Mexico for the first time, making the difficult but essential journey to London to claim in person from the United States embassy there a green card won by me in the American government's oddly raffish immigration lottery. Lucky. I will be able to legally stay in America with Mary. The good thing about CFS is that it does not declare itself when the embassy doctor examines me. I return to America holding in my hand, as required of new immigrants, a big envelope containing an X-ray that proves I am free of tuberculosis. Mary meets me at Albuquerque airport, then leaves me resting on a public bench in Santa Fe while she goes to find her husband.

When she returns, she says, "It's OK. You can come home now." She looks tired, but is smiling.

With reasoning I do not wish to imagine, and which she does not share, she has so well convinced her husband that it is right for me to live with his errant wife and his beloved daughter that his friendliness toward me never wavers.

I do not wish to imagine Mary's reasoning because it might include my harmlessness, my neediness, my disqualification by illness from consideration as a rival, or my ability to share the bills and help support his child. She reveals only that he conceded the negotiation with the words: "All right, I'll give you him."

Or perhaps she said to him with force what she suggests to me softly: that she loves me and wants it to be forever. Or perhaps she simply asserted fiercely that we were determined lovers and that nothing could prevent us, so that he would do well to bend gracefully to the force of our passion. But I think not.

While I was away Mary has left the village and moved sixty miles away to the little rented house we noticed earlier, outside of Santa Fe. She has stuffed it with her books and furniture, and Zoe's toys. The kitchen is fully stocked; Mary's fossil collection lines the windowsills; her family pictures are framed and in place, including one of me, as if I've always been there.

We lack a bed, and Mary has rented a big one and had it installed in the bedroom. I did not know that beds could be rented. There is space for little else. When I arrive, I go there first, collapsing into its embrace. It's the place where I will spend my time. At its foot is a window with a view of the high desert scrub and the hills beyond.

This, I know, is what I now want for my life: a bed at its center, a distant view, love surrounding.

In the mornings Mary rises early to work at her desk before Zoe stirs, bringing to me a cup of hot tea, placing it on the bedside table next to my head, relaxing me into a morning smile, the aching difficulty of the nights falling away. A kiss.

All through childhood, my father, the early riser in our house, brought a cup of tea to each of our beds in the morning, before leaving for the factory at six thirty. While the tea cooled to sipping temperature there was the ticking of his bicycle as he wheeled it from the back garden shed, down the sideway, and into the street, where it joined the tinkle of milk bottles being set on doorsteps, the whir of the milkman's electric cart. Morning tea was love, and home.

On some days Mary comes and sits by me, lightly clothed in a thin robe, lingering in lingerie, taking my proffered hand. If we make love it is then, in early morning, before the effort of the day has spent me. I need to make a wretched calculation, setting love expressed against the ruination of the day. If we make love, I will be left in pain, useless, without any hope of productive work. If we make love in the morning, I will have difficulty in the evening, when it will be my turn to cook or wash dishes to keep up my end of the domestic compact, so that I must calculate which omission threatens more my life with Mary: failure in the love or in the labor.

The little house in the hills outside of Santa Fe is not adobe, not even the facsimile adobe that is legally required within Santa Fe city limits. It is wood walled, tin roofed, rustic with its collapsing porch, cozily located in a spot between low trees and folded hills. It has no name or number, receives no mail, and is located on a dirt road without a name, off another dirt road without a name. We are in America, but off America's map. When I try to explain to a mail order clerk in a distant city that our home has no street address, she refuses to accept that such a place could exist. To achieve the delivery I must first go to the UPS office and draw a map for the driver.

Inside, the house is warm, white, light, and happy. But it is small for three. By the time I arrive there is little space left for me. It is a smallness I would not have accepted in health, to be made so subsidiary and lesser. My few belongings are squeezed in beside Mary's. There is no place for me to work. But my movements have also become small. I no longer have the ability to command or shine, or even to do my share. But I can fit in. In my newly discovered humility, I am grateful.

Mary never rails at my diminishment or uses size against me. There is this secret of hers, that she feels tiny inside. There is her distinctive respect for separateness that I first noticed early with Zoe. There is her own quiet containment, all her inner disturbances kept inner. When she loves, she stands back and loves silently. There is fear in this. One evening, early on, I ask her to join me on the couch to watch TV. I'm not sure cuddling is her style. She hurries over, explaining, when I inquire, that she was unable to join me without an invitation, because she cannot bear rejection. I would not have imagined this.

She keeps candy in jars by the door, plays the piano softly, sets up an enduring game of chess in a quiet corner of the house. We play against each other but never in the other's presence. Sometimes weeks can pass before one of us makes a move, and weeks more before the other notices and thinks to respond. This is Mary: a delightful lightness of connection, an enchanting tenderness, a privacy of thought.

She is even tempered and slow to judge, seemingly untroubled by my illness. She has the desert and the mountains, and hundreds of millions of years of dinosaurs to fill her mind. Men tend to fall in love with her.

I cannot lift Mary, the first lover I cannot lift. I am weak of course, but it is also that she does not want to be lifted. She has a deal with the earth and is disinclined to be swept off it. Although she appears slight, almost willowy, her hips are broad, and beneath her hair her skull is surprisingly large; there is a density of bone in her, a peculiar weight. She explains to me the stone versus bone dispute among paleontologists—some asserting that fossils are essentially bone, others that they are essentially stone—and it is easy to fancy that her inclination toward stone in this debate is expressed in her own skeleton. She is a few inches shorter than me, but I can lean against her.

Mary was brought up among women: mother, grandmother, aunts, sister. She is determinedly vague about the economics of it. Money somehow was there. Her father left them early amid a scandal and to this day denies her existence, a situation she insists does not damage her happiness, and has not much affected her. The female line is strong and she seems to believe that though Zoe might, like her mother, want and enjoy men in her life, she is essentially connected only to Mary. Men are, in the end, subsidiary, and a little suspect.

My world is framed by the window at the bottom of my bed. The branches of a juniper fill the top left corner. In winter the slim branches of a bush—invisible in summer—bend into view under their burden of ice or snow. At certain times the light catches the ice just so, gleaming. The snow piles miraculously high on the thin branches, then sharpens and diminishes each day in the afternoon sun. In summer, pink earth is visible between the cacti, aloe, and desert grasses that were yellow in winter and which turn into a pale green, never bright. The miniature junipers and piñon pines dotting the landscape join to veil the land as it rises up to Apache Ridge, where their sparseness is again revealed. A corner of our neighbor's trailer is just visible between the trees, as are the remains of two old pickups sinking into the ground, already half nature. Migrating birds arrive, heading north, stay awhile, then leave, reappearing months later heading south. A woodpecker pecks at the wood of our house, then moves on. I share all this with Zoe.

This is all a cause for wonder, an immense good fortune. Why then do I count the days of our life together, then the weeks and months, as if they are achievement, not life, as if an end to them is always threatening? I am holding my breath.

Settlers III: How to Be a Communist

You're like Che Guevara," Ben says, bless him. "He had asthma, you know, but it did not stop him doing what he believed in. He couldn't breathe but still went into the hills to fight."

I am on his white couch in Santa Fe, stretched out with my eyes closed, talking, comfortable in a comfortable room, the afternoon sun streaming through large windows. Ben, an old communist, has brought me lemonade and placed it by my head.

Of the Americans I know, he may be the one I most want to be like in my seventies. Though this seems unlikely, since his seventies were earned in his twenties.

He is silver haired, moves quickly, is easily delighted. A lightness in life. Aren't communists supposed to be grim? Aren't they supposed to have lost? The phone rings off the hook for him and Hannah.

"That's an honor," I say, "that I don't deserve." I don't feel heroic. I don't feel like a revolutionary fish swimming in the sea of the people. I feel beached, and thrashing feebly. My daily concerns are for health, love, money and the ability to write a little, with only the content of the writing aspiring to any larger social purpose.

They'd been communists in California first. He'd been a young professor of history at Berkeley in the fifties, and refused, on principle, to sign the McCarthyite pledge the university had demanded.

He'd gone to central Los Angeles instead, to teach in inner city high schools, organize unions and work for civil rights with African Americans. He met Hannah there, doing the same, already with a couple of mixed-race kids in tow. "My god," he says, "it was a lot more interesting than teaching white kids at Berkeley!" It was all good, the organizing, the struggle, even the arrests, even the popular hatred of his ideals. The rights of it were daylight clear: poor people were suffering, nonwhites were discriminated against, and the common-sense answer was for them to organize and pry a larger share from the undeserving rich. Simple justice. He saw, he understood, he acted, in an undivided human flow. All unselfish. An old communist working for America. Happy and at ease. The hatred has not touched him.

They'd ditched the Soviets early when the bad news about that state came out, but they had never wavered in their principles. The work itself had life in it and every day was reward. Discouragement was silly, when helping people made you happy. They spent a lifetime working for others and, to their delight, ended up with decent pensions, thanks to the teaching unions they'd supported.

When Ben turned seventy, they came to Santa Fe, the mountains and the light, and set up home in a development of fake-adobe houses of the type the city's rich Anglo immigrants despised for the lack of Hispanic provenance. But they loved it, the view, the space, the garden, the bright rooms. They loved it every day, and so much wanted it to last that on a visit to Romania they'd taken the chance to be injected with communist monkey glands to prolong their lives, laughing at themselves.

But retire? Hell, no. From what? From life? There was much to be done in Santa Fe too. Ben has his own radio show on local affairs, and Hannah has hers on books. He teaches at the local community college and is organizing a union. She runs the local chapter of the national writers organization and petitions for human rights around the world. They put their efforts into the Green Party, as the pragmatic choice for progress now that socialism is cowed, and see it grow into a local political power. The phone rings off the hook, and when it is answered they are cheery and efficient, helping the fuzzy minded and well meaning to get things done. At their kitchen table I share their cheap and simple convenience foods—no time for fuss about the latest fads or organic purity. They are too busy for purity, taking too much pleasure in activity to be gourmands. In June the Christmas paper napkins are still in use.

Ben gives me the benefit of the doubt. I tell him what I'd seen of the damage done to poor people in poor countries by the interests of the rich in rich countries, the resentments building there, and why the poor are turning to Islam rather than to Marx. And how I had become unable to find a principled place for myself in international aid. We can talk, connect, and share regret that misery is spread so wide in service of rewards so tawdry and unsatisfying. We can agree on the forces that drive all this, good old-fashioned Marxian analysis, still with merit if not currency. But when he urges me to be more involved, I evade. I have the excuse of illness.

But the truth is I have never been good at joining. Unlike Ben and Hannah, my understanding does not flow naturally into effective action. I remained hesitant, never quite convinced, clinging to independence, and suffering an uncompleted human flow, progress halted in the mind. This cannot be healthy.

A good life, his, I think. Unselfish, useful, brave and happy. A good marriage, full of love and appreciation, feeding on the life outside, not on each other. No thought for money, yet incidentally ending well enough. Accidentally spiritual, by giving freely, by delight in life, by forgetting himself. Accidentally light. Accidentally heroic.

I try "heroic" for myself, stretched out, eyes closed, on their new white couch in the sunlight, trying to see myself as Che, the way Ben has offered, but it seems all wrong.

Illness as Metaphor

She catches a cold on the subway
Her immune system is depressed
Well, her boss is a bully.

A meteorite crashes through the roof
He is never the same again
What can you expect with that childhood?

She is hit by a speeding car crossing the road
Where is her agility today?
If only she had not broken up with her boyfriend.

Your cancer?
Is it the food you ate, the drugs you took, the stress you courted?
Or the filthy world you live in?
Does it stand for all this?
Are you to blame?

Your depression
Your fault by default
Since it's in your mind
Isn't it?
The disability companies say so
Not paying out
Parsing for profit
Carving separation of body and mind into law.

CFS
Is hysteria
According to Elaine Showalter
A literary critic
Who therefore asserts that
It's just an expression
Like false memories and alien abduction
Of cultural anxiety
She trumpets this view
And receiving hate mail
Wonders at it prettily.

There is a tendency in books
This one too
To give false meaning to illness
It's hard to describe the truth
And keep to it
When so much metaphor
Is so cheaply available.

He will fall
And then will rise
Wiser
A good story.

Love at Last: Zoe

What I like best about Zoe at seven is the way she backs away from the cartoons on weekend TV, a bowl of Cheerios in her hands, and transfixed by what she sees, without even looking toward me, or even noticing me, navigates her way back to my knee and sits on it, her bony bottom digging into my thigh, making herself comfortable, as if I am furniture.

In the first days we tussled ridiculously over the front seat of Mary's car. Zoe, at six, thought the place next to her mother should be hers, and I wanted it to be mine. Mary, in her way, stayed aloof. I strained to keep my dignity, but when I did, I always lost to Zoe, who did not know the meaning of it. She dashed for the car door and belted herself in, turning to give me a smirk of victory while I reconciled myself to being a backseat adult, second class. I volunteered to drive, even when I was not well enough to drive, to avoid this humiliation.

Then, suddenly, it does not matter to her anymore. Now Zoe likes me sitting next to Mary, likes Mary and me.

She has a generous heart, room for me and her father. Sometimes she pushes me across the room, like a heavy chess piece, then pushes her mother toward where I stand until we collide, embrace, laugh. She then regards her handiwork with satisfaction, then wriggles between us. "My family," she says.

I learn about toys for little girls—the variety of Polly Pocket sets, for example—what is in vogue for them, what is cool this month and what is not. I recall, and honor, from my own childhood, the glamour attached to books and toys assigned to the next age up, the ones currently blessed by Zoe's goddess friends of eight. In Toys R Us, I effortlessly store in my mind—which otherwise refuses to reliably store—the items that catch Zoe's interest, producing them as presents on birthdays and Christmas. She is an easy child; she rarely pleads for anything.

From my bed, where I am making a long afternoon study of the ceiling, I overhear Zoe talking outside to her friend, two years her elder. The friend is the little girl from the trailer next door who had hooked onto me recently, since her sweet, but alcoholic, father has been exiled from home by his wife and made to live in a shed. The two of them are upping the ante on what the adults in their lives can do, climb on roofs, solve this and that, drive up perilous mountain tracks, keep awake all hours. Then I hear six-year-old Zoe declare of me, "He can do anything!" and after thoughtful consideration her eight-year-old friend concedes, "Yes, he can." I laugh at the sweetness of it; I can do anything this afternoon, but stand.

Each night I must carry Zoe to her bath. Upside down, by her ankles, giggling. Though Mary sometimes says, "Leave him alone, Zoe, he's tired today," I must do it. As she progresses from five to eight, it takes more effort. Sometimes I lose the whole next day because of this evening effort, but still I must do it. I carry Zoe to her bath and afterward Mary reads her to sleep. Zoe has a right to these certainties, as proof of love.

By habit, before school, Zoe visits me where I lie in bed listening to my portable radio—a survivor from my English life, intended then for listening to weather forecasts at sea—and nursing the cooling cup of tea Mary has made for me. Mary's big black cat arrives first, and is already a heavy lump on my legs. Zoe takes the space vacated by her mother and chats sagaciously about her best friends, and why they are. While we talk, Mary drifts in and out with her lovely morning habit of padding around in her underwear while contemplatively considering the day, and the clothes for it.

On a day when I am feeling well, Zoe and I walk up a nearby mountain stream together where the water is low. Arthur, our new big-nosed, big-pawed puppy, splashes around us. There are no footpaths here and Mary has taught me to walk in water, a paleontologist's way of traveling unmarked landscapes in warm climates. Our shoes are soaked but it does not matter. This is sunny New Mexico, not dank England. We step from rock to rock and wade shallow pools, crossing under the one-track railway on our way to find the donkey who lives upstream. Zoe is game, but I make her dare too much jumping between two wet rocks. I see at the last moment that she will not make it and with a speed and certainty that can only come from love, I launch myself forward so that when she lands it is on me, not rock, soft and safe, me laughing at my cuts and bruises so as not to frighten her.

Later on, Zoe and I, just the two of us, fly to Los Angeles together to meet Mary's sister, Zoe with her little backpack carefully stocked with reliable pleasures. We line up at the airport desk together and for the first—and only—time I do the special early boarding for parents with children. I am a parent, and proud. I am bursting with it. On the plane, Zoe decisively folds up the armrest between us and snuggles up to me in sleep.

We've picked out Arthur, the three of us, from a litter of fat golden puppies with big black noses, who are the unwanted offspring of a pedigreed golden retriever gone bad with a very large interloper, Great Pyrenees, we think. He's the biggest puppy, the most curious and most comic, and we choose him. Zoe names him and I try it out: "Hello, my Arthur," I say. "He's not just yours," Zoe corrects sharply. "He belongs to all of us."
"Yes," I agree, "all of us."

Doctor XI: Not a Real Doctor

Among the not-real doctors are Treeleaf the Reiki practitioner, who moves her hands over me at a safe distance, molding electricity from the air; Mr. Chou, the old Chinese man who has me filling the house with vile smells of stewing herbs; and Lila, the lesbian acupuncturist. Lila is the one who sticks.

I lie down and relax while she darts long, thin needles into me, which waver there like bulrushes, or lights tiny herbal bonfires on me. I'm happy to have things done to me, since this requires no effort.

Lila talks. "You'd be surprised how much therapy goes down here," she says, though most of the talk is hers. She is burly with dyke hair and a gap-toothed smile. "Adrenal overload," she declares offhandedly for a diagnosis, which medical tests of my adrenal function later prove to be quite accurate.

She's can-do, and has done. Keen not to follow the feminine path, she previously had a career in silver mining in Colorado. She took the most dangerous jobs, located at the bottom of cliffs being blasted away from the top, only giving it up when proof of the mine owners' casual attitude toward human life was serially confirmed. "By then, I'd got some of the anger out of me," she says. "I was ready to heal, and to heal others." I find myself chuckling at her story. This is what delights me about America: that it is not judged ridiculous for a woman to jump from blasting silver ore to alternative health care.

Lila charges her clients according to the cars they drive up in. She soaks the Range Rover crowd and assigns my Japanese pickup a bargain price. With the money I am saving by having no health insurance, I can afford to have these not-real doctors.

We discuss our love lives, the difficulty with long-term fidelity, the problematic lure of pretty girls. She's in a relationship too, but is finding her irrepressible nature to be difficult to repress. Mary, she notes, is quite something. She's inclined to a mischievous grin, and has recently given her smile a more diabolical edge by adding gold teeth because she rather likes Mike Tyson's look.

I tend to go quiet toward the end of our sessions, finding a profound relaxation in Lila's confident presence and the waving fields of needles emerging from me. I am the earth.

Each time I leave Lila I am refreshed, with more energy than when I arrived, and for some time this convinces me of the healing power of acupuncture. But as the visits continue, I notice something else: that the increase in energy is paid for by a corresponding dip later in the day. Apparently acupuncture moves my energy around but does not increase it, or address any cause. But I continue to see Lila because I like our sessions.

Her partner is offered a job in Bangladesh, and she wonders whether she would be happy there. "Go," I say, forever recommending travel to others. "Bangladesh is surprisingly beautiful," I tell her, and explain that I've never forgotten the roads crammed with brightly colored saris and rickshaws, the expansive luminous green of the rice fields next to them, and in the distance the white sails of boats gliding between fields on hidden rivers. I also say that it seemed to me, when I worked there—advising on jute production then—that the white people, the expats, lived good lives, comfortable and happy. I see a fire light up in her eyes at my descriptions.

In her letter months after her departure for Dhaka, I learn that things are not so good for Lila in Bangladesh. It's hard for her to find useful work, and people are put off by her gold-toothed grin. Her overflowing energy is considered rude in an overcrowded place, where smallness is polite. In big America her extroversion had been admired, and was the way to make room for an unconventional life, so that she now confesses to confusion. Then there are the other whites there. The foreign community has sniffed at an American out-there, can-do dyke, never mind the goodness of her heart. It seems I do not think long enough before offering my advice.

Love at Last: Continued

This, then, is why I came to America, isn't it? To find love and family, the heart of a new life.

After Zoe has been bathed and has been read to sleep, Mary and I sip gin and tonics, mine without the gin. A single sip of alcohol jazzes my neural chemistry into comprehensive disarray, a marker, it seems, for CFS. I lie down on the couch and Mary sits by me. Zoe sleeps nearby in her room, the door open. We turn the lights down low and our breathing settles into unity. Outside is the clear, starry night of the New Mexico mountains. Coyotes howl, but we are snug. Quiet people, touching, appreciative of something tender in the other.

"What are you thinking?" I ask Mary.
"I always hate it when people ask that," she replies, then laughs a little and relents. "I was feeling grateful."

We've stepped into our relationship with a new life fully formed, without the usual preparations, and we've been immediately grateful. Though I am sometimes cranky with illness, there has never been a serious argument. Mary is disinclined to argue. She prefers to demur. She is also disinclined to talk of love, believing that the proof of it is not in words but in a quiet obedience to its form. Her past failures in love, she intimates, have been in the failures of men to properly appreciate her.

Mary's preoccupations speed backward, past her present life and the pull of recent history, past her childhood and straight back to the time of dinosaurs, where she feels most safe.

Our days are like walking a tightrope into a mist, counting steps, uncertain whether there is a far side to reach. I don't know why I feel like this.

My world grows larger with time and rest. The window at the bottom of the bed is less its frame. I've come to know the dirt road near our house as a small animal close to the ground might know it. Twice a day I range one or two hundred yards in one direction or the other with puppy Arthur for company. Sometimes Zoe comes too, less often Mary. Usually it's just me and Arthur. I become familiar with the miniature topography of my limited territory, the road's rain-scoured gullies, arroyos, and mesas, scaled for rodents. One large pink rock emerges proud enough to threaten the undersides of our cars, and I pay this special attention, as to a major landmark. My body knows the road's gradients and their precise demands, which determine the direction and duration of our outings.

The views from the high spots are imprinted on me, the mists and sunsets. I stand still to look down at our little house at dusk, the yellow light in its windows showing through the trees, our two modest cars nuzzling in the clearing. Inside, I know, Mary is moving about in her bathrobe, slowly, gracefully, efficiently, ready to welcome my return with a smile, while Zoe, in her bathrobe, is ready to fly at my legs.

Arthur, I tell them proudly, on my return, has learned a trick: to trot across the bars of the cattle grid without any of his four paws missing its footing, a talent he will never lose. He seems, I report, pleased with himself, but unsurprised at his brilliance.

When I can, I write, a loose longhand, while propped up in bed with pillows. I cannot sit upright at a desk for more than a few minutes, and the effort of holding my arms over a keyboard is entirely prohibitive. I try to lead my brain away from New Mexico, to Zanzibar. In my writing I am a lively, Arab Asian woman, far from Santa Fe and illness. I am struggling to leave the oppressive island in search of a bigger, freer life. I am an ingenious young entrepreneur, sexy, irrepressible, bound for big things, love and trouble. I am set on a migrant's path, to London, then maybe on to America. The worst health I experience is a cough.

My writing is often feeble in both imagination and penmanship. Instead of typing my drafts, I dictate them onto cassette tapes and pay someone to type from them. When the typist's son accidentally wipes my tapes clean, I don't feel very much sense of loss.

Still, I am doing more these days. I am walking more, working more. On a visit to Los Alamos I briefly join in the ice skating with Zoe and Mary. My mind draws a graph of my future health in which the daily variations are averaged, and the trend reaches up into a busy, prosperous, normal future.

We need more prosperity now, since we are living on diminishing savings. Mary's research funding has ended, but instead of finding more she is continuing to do what she loves, as if money is an optional reality. She has a secret dinosaur, up in the mountains, something her paleontology competitors must not learn of before she has excavated it. In her past the money has always come. Her needs are not extravagant. The childhood was mysteriously provided for, there have been grants acquired through adoring professors, a home supplied by her husband, a little inheritance, and now there is me. Now it is up to me to treasure her.

I muse aloud, just once, whether, given my infirmity, she might not be the one to seek a full-time job, and see her step back, bridling with a shocked refusal that she does not need to speak, but which I take to say: How dare you; you have the gift of me; I have the care of Zoe; your part is clear.

Skating at Los Alamos

We ice skate at Los Alamos, among the atomic bombers.

The rink is underutilized, like everything there, just some gangly PhDs with their families, the men bespectacled and bearded, no dress sense, the women suburban moms from anywhere. We sing Christmas carols there too, attend the birthday parties of the children.

Years before, on my first visit to New Mexico, I drove the sixty miles there alone one night, before I knew a soul. I was unsure whether it was possible to drive into Los Alamos, and had expected to be stopped and questioned, or to reach a checkpoint like the ones at army bases. I was drawn on and up into the mountain night by the pleasure of apprehension. What might be expected from a place whose sole reason for existence was the research of nuclear weapons in remote isolation, and on whose collective conscience rested Hiroshima and Nagasaki?

The rock cuts beside the road up the mountain from Española looked fresh in the headlights, the road surface too smooth for the region's poverty. When I breasted the ridge and drifted down into the city center, I found a nighttime ghost city, modern, neat, empty, a suburb in the sky, a closed McDonald's squatting there with its glassy spaceship glow. I circled around, the only vehicle, passing miles of tight wire fences broken by the entrances to boldly labeled facilities, Area 64, Area 41, and so on, all floodlit, all deserted, all humming. Effectively sinister.

No enduring human logic would seed a city here. There's no river for irrigating an agriculture, no natural crossroad for travelers or trade, the usual itches for cities. At most, it might have supported a remote outpost village with some special deal with nature, harvesting firewood, for example, or summer grazing, or perhaps a cache of minerals to justify a mine. This sense of falseness continued, to my mind, in the banality of the suburban homes with their architectures lifted from other parts of America, and in the presence of familiar shops and chain restaurants, which, I theorized, must have been bribed by government to locate here in order to provide a semblance of normality.

On this first visit, I carried my preconception with me—that Los Alamos was sinister—came at night, and found confirmation everywhere. I felt certain that my car was monitored by many cameras, and after the last of several U-turns in front of the forbidding gates of numbered research facilities, I spooked myself enough to dive for the road back out of town and to speed down the mountain to the overlooked, poor, rough, defiantly Hispanic town of Española, sitting where a town should sit, on a river, the Rio Grande, a town I associated with low incomes, and a blessed humanity that even at this late hour patrolled in low-rider cars with illuminated undercarriages, young men slowly cruising the main street for small-time honest trouble.

The second time I visit Los Alamos is with Mary and Zoe, to a children's birthday party, a bright afternoon of Jell-O followed by fireworks at dusk, and the laughter and tears of six-year-olds.

Mary, it turns out, has visiting scientist rights at the National Laboratory, access to some of their equipment, and friendships among the geologists up there. To her, Los Alamos is a useful resource in a part of the world otherwise deficient in scientists. She and other outsiders are being courted, now the cold war has collapsed and the future for atomic bombs is looking bleak. Los Alamos is scrambling for a new identity that will support it and keep the money coming in, arguing, for example, that it is well placed to be at the forefront of environmental research. The forbidding secrecy will be replaced by open doors, sunshine and smiles. It does not last, of course, this panic toward the light; new fears will be identified and a need for America to defend itself with new advances in nuclear weaponry discovered and funded. The new-old atmosphere of enemies, weapons and secrecy will be restored, and, to celebrate this return, a Taiwanese scientist will be falsely accused of espionage when he takes his work home.

At the Christmas carol evenings in the homes of physicists, conversation is truncated. They are friendly, these scientists, quick to offer food and drink, but are unwilling to talk about their work and are uncomfortable with more general subjects. Their lives are lived in too remote a place. What is left to them is a cheesy jokiness carried over from long years as graduate students in university science departments, and a declared interest in TV sport. Many, though, are serious and hearty in the singing of carols.

I push at them, wanting to know more, just slightly the bully, casting myself as the freer man. They are diminished, I hint, to the degree they are obliged to conceal their views. At the very least, are they not entitled to their own opinions on matters of defense and technology, and are they not obliged, being uniquely qualified to speak, to stand up for what they believe? They offer drinks, dip their heads, and move away. More rarely, because generally they do not think of it, they turn the tables on me to ask me what I do, then find themselves awkward with both literature and poverty in foreign places, each taken to be irrelevant to what is truly important.

I lie down on couches all over Los Alamos, while Mary satisfies her requirement for the company of scientists. At a busy wedding reception at the house of a senior scientist, my low tolerance for the effort of company is soon overwhelmed and I seek a couch in quiet solitude, finding a cool leather one in the office of our host, located in a distant wing of his house. I close the door and put up my feet.

For an hour or two I lie there quite still, in my customary state of semiconscious recuperation. Then, as I reanimate, my eyes focus on the rows of neat, dusted files and on the lights of the desktop computers, and I consider where I am. This quiet office is some sort of inner sanctum, and what it is an inner sanctum of, is the world's most potent and deadly enterprise, the determination of America to dominate through nuclear intimidation. From what is created here in Los Alamos, American power flows, and everything that is carried with it. This is its quiet center. And through the coincidence of love and illness, I am here too, an outsider, a foreigner, with quite other interests—more general ones. I understand, through the gauze of illness, that this is an opportunity unlikely to be repeated, and that I might find a rare insight, a telling detail, or at the least a good story—material—by flicking through the files, or nudging the computers off their screen savers onto something more revealing.

I think this but in the end I do not act on it. I have the nerve—fear of consequence demands a pitch of nervous activity that I can no longer indulge—and I could overcome my misgivings at the discourtesy of prying on my host, but in the end I just cannot summon the energy. My eyes do not want to scan, my brain does not want to analyze, my body does not want to stand up and reach for files or sit at a desk. So, I think I'll let it pass, unique opportunity or not, for the sake of lying down a little longer, flattened at the center of America.

How to Get a Job

First of all, you don't tell them you are sick.

This seems fair because you're getting better, and you expect to be completely well by the time the job begins. You believe this. And, besides, you need the job and there are two hundred applicants.

Mary drives you to Albuquerque airport and puts you on a plane with a lingering tender touch, so that you feel you are lying for three.

In San Francisco you take a taxi straight to the hotel the university has booked, check in, and lie down. You have three hours of lying perfectly still before dinner with some faculty. You do not know San Francisco but you do not even consider going outside.

You're doing OK at dinner. You can feel it in your legs, threatening, but it stays back like a weak neap tide. You talk quietly and not too much. You sit composed in your chair, not draining energy by leaning forward eagerly, or by demonstrating animation. You are keeping meticulous energy accounts.

Later you discover that the faculty—mainly female—liked this: a modest, soft-spoken man who did not assert his importance.

It is explained that the department has pursued the university policy of diversity in gender, race and sexual orientation to good effect. As it happens, they are now short of a heterosexual white man. They fall into a departmental politics discussion among themselves: apparently there is a problem in that the woman hired to fill a bisexual slot has been having sex only with men. There is some bad feeling.

You are warned by two of the women faculty that if hired you must never, never have an affair with a female student. Later you discover that both are living with younger men who were once their students.

It's your birthday. You admit this when you accidentally pull out of your pocket the handmade card that Zoe gave you. The women are enchanted by her picture of you; it proves to be your best move.

Everyone is drinking, but you do not drink. The wine is generally praised as exceptional. As the evening progresses the table falls into louder and more contentious departmental arguments and they forget about you. Nobody notices that you are sitting motionless.

The next day is crucial. In addition to interviews you must teach a writing workshop while observed by twenty faculty. Normally this would make you very nervous but you understand that, in the absence of adrenaline, anxiety will make you ill rather than alert, so you excuse yourself from care.

You begin the day by eating a full cooked breakfast at a diner near the hotel. You must not run out of calories. Then you discover that you have inadvertently walked downhill and must now walk back up. The effort crashes you. Your feet are dragging, your brain fogging. By ten in the morning you are losing all abilities and the class is not until four in the afternoon. You lie down. Very still.

By one, you are increasingly troubled by your inability to make a decision: You want to stimulate yourself by drinking a rare—and therefore potent—cup of coffee before going to the university. It's time to smash the doctors' rules. However, the hotel has no room service or cafe. To get the cup of coffee, you will need to walk to and from the diner, the same effort that drove you down into collapse in the morning. It's a hard call. You decide not to go. You put on a tie and lie down again, waiting to be picked up.

At the university they immediately offer you coffee. You say, "Please," as if you did this every day. The class goes amazingly well. You sit down throughout, making yourself an equal among the graduate students, who are arranged in a circle around a table. When they introduce themselves you write down their names on a table plan, knowing you will not otherwise remember a single one. Later you are congratulated on your recall, and the use of the students' names. The students are also under scrutiny. You conspire together a pleasant, cooperative discussion. Afterward you are told that an earlier candidate offended them with his ebullience, which was judged overbearing.

You are driven back to the hotel and decline an evening invitation that seems like politeness. You lie down, everything tingling with tiny alarm bells.

The next day you are driven to the airport by one of the women faculty, who hints that you're in with a chance. You may, in fact, have it in the bag. They really didn't like that other, overbearing man, never mind his résumé. She brings up the gap in your résumé, the last two years when you said you had been simply writing.
You decide it's best to put down a marker for the truth: "Actually, my health went through a bad patch."
"You're better now?"
"Getting there."
"Something from your years in the tropics?"
"Probably," you say.
"One thing about working here," she says, "is the great benefits, especially the health insurance. San Francisco is expensive and the salaries aren't wonderful, but there is that."
She's selling you the job. You relax.

Two weeks later, when you are formally offered the job, you say you cannot accept it. It turns out that Zoe cannot leave New Mexico until the divorce is complete and Mary's husband agrees.

"That's courageous," Mary says to me quietly when I tell her, having stayed out of my decision. She risks giving me a rare kiss. We kiss often; what is rare is Mary risking the initiative.

The women in San Francisco are unexpectedly sympathetic to my situation, or perhaps disinclined to endure more interviews. In any case, they do not accept my refusal. They will keep the position for me for a year. Now I have a better chance to recover before I go. On the other hand, honor now dictates that I absolutely must go.

Doctor XII: Thumper

My new doctor, I'll discover down the road from yet another doctor, has a nickname. "Oh, old Thumper," he will say, a smile spreading. "I know him." In answer to my unspoken query, he adds, "That's what we used to call him at medical school, Thumper."
"Why?"
He shrugs, still smiling. Thumper is clearly the sort of joke you cannot share with a patient.
"And how," he will ask sardonically, "is old Thumper doing in Santa Fe?"

Thumper has a new alternative medicine practice in Santa Fe, a new office, and outside, a new red BMW with crash damage. Someone has judged it worthwhile to invest in a young alternative doctor in a city rich in alternative women. Shirley MacLaine is their present leader. I am one of Thumper's first patients, and I never see another man in his office.

There is about Thumper something comic. It's hard to put your finger on it—his straining for authority perhaps, his unconvincing sternness, or his shifty refusal to meet your eye. I feel it, and others feel it too. His new car is too obvious, and he's already crashed it. The enduring lack of repair during the period he treats me suggests a general incompetence with care.

He is a short man, compact, sandy haired, good looking in a featureless way. Early thirties. A bit of a jock, I'd guess, from his walk, his tan, and the skis on his roof rack. More at home, I decide, in the après-ski bars than in the caring industries. Something about him brings out the bully in me. At our first meeting I ask him about the no scent policy posted on his door, given that he is himself scented. He huffs and fidgets, then does not answer, but makes it clear that he will ask the questions here. There is something about this performance that makes me want to incite it again. I think of that insignificant bird that puffs up its chest hugely in its mating dance, gaining size but not dignity.

By the time I first enter Thumper's office, I am no longer a passive recipient of advice from expert doctors. My many doctors have, after all, achieved nothing in three years. I am on my way to becoming a skeptical consumer of health care, a newly assertive patient with a growing sense that doctors habitually pretend to wisdom they don't possess, and that I might now know more than them.

I lay out my analysis and ask him if this matches his understanding of CFS. He demurs, avoids, shifts, hedges, suggests repeating some tests. "Well," I press, "can you do enzyme potentiated desensitization or not? It's the reason I've come to you." EPD is an elaborate treatment I have read about in a book my mother sent me from England, and for which a high rate of success is reported. I find the theory behind it very convincing.

We talk about money. His practice is new and empty. He decides to do it.

And that's all there is to Doctor XII. He does what I ask, takes my money, and never much likes me.

Pregnant

Mary says, "I have something to tell you. I know we did not plan for this, but it seems to be true. I'm pregnant. We've been taking chances."

We're standing in the middle of our living room on a Saturday morning. Zoe is with her father this weekend.

I know what I am supposed to do. I am supposed to show my spontaneous joy and reassure Mary that this is what I want more than anything, that I love her, and that everything will work out fine. I know this is what I am supposed to do. I look at her, then take her in my arms so that I am looking not at Mary, but staring across the room behind her, saying nothing.

I am in fact leaning on Mary, because I am suddenly drenched with a wash of utter despair. This is what I've long wanted—what the old healthy self long wanted—more than anything in the world: a child. New life. I want to love unselfishly, uncomplicatedly, unreservedly, and make something good of that. I want to see the world afresh through my child's eyes, as I do with Zoe. I want the comforting extent of family. But CFS is not sharing this desire at all. It rejects unreservedly any tiny bit of additional effort. It has had enough of my imposing my will and desires on my body, thank you very much. It's making this point, even now, by removing all muscular support and no longer pumping blood to my brain, which collaborates by absolutely forbidding any attempt to reorganize itself to accommodate this big new fact. It isn't letting me convincingly articulate the words that a hundred films and novels have conditioned me to say: "That's wonderful, darling."

Instead, I say, "I need to lie down." When lying down, I say, "We'll manage." Mary is looking down at me as if she's seeing me for the first time and not particularly liking what she sees. I'm having difficulty meeting her eye. I say, "It's because of something like this that I didn't want you to give up your health insurance," as if it is this that is the problem. I also want to say that I wish she would earn some money and not leave everything to me, doesn't she know I'm ill? I manage to hold that one back. I have some sense of what she's hearing, which is that I'm not sure I want to be bound to her by a child, that I might want to leave instead. Her greatest fear.

Mary has stepped back, as if I'd raised my hand to her. I shouldn't have mentioned the health insurance. Criticisms like this are why she left her husband. Now she's leaving the bedroom. I've failed in the love and reassurance response.

I stay flat, looking at the ceiling, while my heart tries to find a rhythm. I can't find a way through this. I want a child more than anything. CFS, currently in charge of my body and mind, doesn't want it at all. After an hour or so, when rest has restored some energy to me, I still don't have the right words for Mary. What I have for her is an embrace and the words, "I think I should go out for a drive to work this out. Don't worry, OK?"
"Do what you have to do," she replies.

To the north of us are country roads, passing old, left-behind Hispanic towns. I stop in one for a bowl of chili, then on leaving the restaurant, I turn right, not left, continuing north away from home. I'm in Colorado by the time I lose it and find I can't go on, or back. At a cheap motel I lean against the reception desk and complain ineffectually to the Indians about the price, the way I do when I've lost my mind.

Later, I call Mary from the motel pay phone and explain where I am and that my health has crashed.

She's reserved. "You got so far?"

"I'll drive back tomorrow," I tell her. "I'll be better then. Everything will be OK."

I can't sleep. I watch terrible TV through the night. *Buffy the Vampire Slayer*.

In the morning, I am able to drive again. My bloated brain occupies itself with deciding which road to take, and I hope it is sorting out fatherhood in its back rooms. It seems important to make a circle of my journey rather than retrace the route of my shameful flight. I choose an old mountain road.

On the dirt road I have a puncture and limp into the nearest settlement. A group of bikers are the only people I can see on the run-down main street. At a makeshift garage, an elderly mechanic tries to make a deal with me. He can change the wheel and repair the puncture, if I jack up the car and remove the wheel myself. I gather from his Spanish-laced English that his back is no good. Otherwise, I'll have to wait until the afternoon when he might have some help. I think about it and I am certain that the effort of jacking up the car will collapse me. If I try, I will have a functioning vehicle, but will be unable to drive home.

The old man can't understand my problem. I look OK. I'm not old and bent like him. I can only be an Anglo so surpassingly lazy and inept that I'd rather waste half a day than jack up my own car. He's disgusted and is not going to go out of his way to help me. He may not help at all. I lie down on the rough-wood bench outside his garage. I see him talking to the bikers and the bikers looking at me. I close my eyes, trying to even my breath, trying to let my muscles relax, trying to let my mind go blank.

It's midafternoon before the pickup is fixed, and I'm only a few miles out of town when I find I can no longer drive. I back off the narrow road onto the bank of a stream, open up the cap of the pickup, and lie down inside on the foam mattress I keep there for this purpose. I lie quite still, letting the brook's chatter run through me. It would be nice if the brook was working things out for me. What does tireless water make of pregnancy? A small, ordinary thing, nothing too much to worry about?

The sky turns black and lightning strikes close by, the thunder crashing violently enough to rock the truck. Rain beats a furious percussion on its roof. I relax into a gorgeous surrender to nature. I like the enormity of it and the sense that it could wash me away or strike me dead. I can do nothing. I am responsible for nothing. The rain beats into the open back of the truck, soaking my feet, which I do not attempt to move. It's just not worth the effort. I don't want any more effort. I just want to stay horizontal while things happen to me.

I must have passed out. The storm has gone, but the day is still overcast. The stream has grown into a torrent, not chattering now, but elbowing past rocks with a jostling urgency. But I'm calm. My brain has cooled and opened like a flower. The storm and rest have inexplicably restored me. Of course I want our child! Now that I am able to drive, it's a matter of urgency to get home to Mary before it's too late. I may have lost her already, and my child. I can see the future now. In the future I will be well. I drive over the mountain passes at breakneck speed, flashing my lights until slower vehicles pull over to let me pass.

Safe back at home, after I've garbled my explanation for the lost day, I say, holding her, "It's all right. I'm sorry I needed to leave. I just felt overwhelmed. I'm sorry. I don't know how we will do this, but we will. I want this more than anything."

She holds me in return. And holds back too.

Two weeks later she calls me from the conference she is attending at Ghost Ranch. "I've had a miscarriage," she says.

"I'm so sorry," I respond, my heart flying out to her. "Are you all right?" But she's telling me the anecdotal detail, about how she had been giving a paper when the blood started running down her thigh, and how she'd had to rush out. She's laughing at it. And she says, "I'm fine." Relief and loss are pitching a nauseating battle in me.

"I'm coming to stay with you," I say. "I'll bring Zoe." Mary says she'd like that. When we arrive she's delighted to see us. She's enjoying her work and the public recognition. She's almost jaunty.

Years later, I have lunch with an old friend of Mary's, who says in passing, ". . . just after the abortion."
"You mean the miscarriage," I quickly correct her.
The friend looks down at the tablecloth, then concurs, "Yes, of course, the miscarriage."

And after that I no longer know. I'd forgotten how good Mary was at secrets. I'd never doubted her for a second. I'd forgotten how our love itself had begun with lies, me dependent on her brilliant duplicity.

Doctor XIV: Definitely Not a Real Doctor

A Frenchwoman, chic, petite, of a *certain age*, arrives uninvited at our door. I've never seen her before. She has heard about me, she says, and that I am ill. She can cure me. She can't remember who gave her my name.

This is wonderful.

Herself, she lives by charity in the guesthouse of a rich person, but still she requires no payment. I will simply need to visit her home at exactly nine each morning for the next five weeks. She is never clear about how she has heard of me.

Mary, in her way, withdraws from the conversation, skeptical according to her smile—of either the treatment or the woman—but unwilling to be influential.

I go as suggested. Why not? I want to believe her. The treatment involves my bare back and the pressing of fingertips at exact points on it, in the particular order demanded by a page of instructions that she holds up with her left hand while pressing me with her right.

She's been taught this treatment in a mountain commune somewhere, which promotes it as a sort of pyramid scheme of health care. You are healed but then must learn the technique and heal others in return. Hence the lack of payment. She has been cured of something. I have the impression that taking care of others does not come naturally to her, but that she feels the pressure of obligation. It works for everything, she asserts, cancer even. What amazes her, she says, is that the teachers in the commune do not take any special care of their health. They are overweight. They smoke. But they are healthy. It's amazing.

While I put my shirt back on, she likes to talk. She has her worries. Certainly. Her tenure in this guesthouse is insecure. You could never tell with rich Americans, no? What they are thinking. Someone wants to displace her, she thinks, and is plotting. The bitch. It is so hard to find suitable work in Santa Fe, don't I think? For a sensitive person. Though it is so special, so magical.

Why is she not back home in France? She does not know why.

Her adobe guesthouse is small but elegant and she had made it exquisite with precious decorations, artworks, fabrics, dried flowers. There is evidence of expensive foods purchased in tiny, thrifty quantities. While she touches me with her fingertips, incense smolders.

We say good-bye after the five weeks of morning visits. She expresses mild puzzlement that I have experienced no beneficial effect at all, and I feel sad to see she is not entirely surprised by this proof of her ineffectuality. She does not doubt the treatment's efficacy, only hers. She continues to refuse any payment and requests nothing more, not even that we keep in touch, assuring me that the treatment might take time to work. I try to cheer her up by agreeing that this is my expectation too, but nothing does change. I never see her again, or hear anything about her.

Leaving Love

You should go on your own," says Mary, the opposite of what she thinks.

I nod in reply, too disturbed in myself to choose words, but also unwilling to contradict her. My departure will end my nervous counting of the days of happiness.

Over a year has passed since I postponed the job in San Francisco. I would like to think that I am more healthy, but it might be only that I rest more. In the year Mary has won her exhausted husband around to the idea of Zoe moving out of the state and has completed the divorce. They are free to come with me.

What Mary wants is to go to San Francisco as a family. I will work at my new job and they will continue as before. Already we have visited Marin County where the schools for Zoe are reputedly better than the ones in the city. We have been stunned by rents so high that they would use up my entire salary.

There is, in the prospect of the move, something that draws up in me an anxiety so persistent that in the end I have to voice it. I'm worried, I tell Mary, that I will not be able to do this job, and that the result will be that we will be living in one of the world's most expensive places without any community or means of support. At the very least, I worry that I will be unable to do my job and also undertake my share of domestic chores and care for Zoe. Mary listens and carefully says nothing. Perhaps it would be more sensible, I wonder aloud, to keep the inexpensive home in New Mexico and keep Zoe in her school until I know whether I can do the job. This is sensible, but I intuit that sense is a weak player in Mary's mind. "You mean," she says, "that Zoe and I stay behind?" "Until I'm settled," I reply.

Friends—but not Mary—put the argument that having Mary and Zoe with me will help me in my work, but I know better. They do not understand. The social effort of a relationship, the conversation, the domestic give and take, the shared meals, the lovemaking: each of these delights is an additional call on my scarce energy, the combination overwhelming. Then there is lovely Zoe, and the attention she needs, and that I would want to give her without calculation. She will not understand a life in which I only work and lie down, with no attention for her. But this conclusion—that I should go alone to concentrate on the new job—is so close to the old habit of running from love that I do not want to accept it.

"You should go alone," says Mary, releasing me. "It's best. We can join you later. You can have Arthur." I am relieved.

Mary makes me a package of one plate, one cup, one knife, one fork, and ties it with pink ribbon, handing it to me just before I leave.

My relief at the shedding of responsibilities is less by Albuquerque, where I stop for a final cheap Mexican meal at the Frontier Cafe.

By Gallup, it is gone entirely.

In Flagstaff, I call home from the Motel 6, but Mary does not pick up the phone. I leave a loving message.

By Needles the pain of loss is sharp.

In Tehachapi, my new aloneness is mixed with the small pleasures of familiarity from staying at the Cactus Motel where I've once stayed with Mary and Zoe.

When, after three days, I make it to the room in the university hotel in San Francisco, where I will stay while looking for a place to rent, I call home and find Mary and Zoe there to tell them I miss them. Mary says evenly that she's pleased I've made it all the way in one piece. She's not one for effusive telephone chat. Zoe wants to know everything about my journey and gives me an update on everything she's done and seen, and the current disposition of Arthur, who is due to join me when I have somewhere to live.

Before I reach my room, and though I am near collapse, I try to get the student receptionist to talk, to smile. I am using the very last of my resources to try to strike up a conversation with the first person I meet in San Francisco. Newly arrived, newly alone, full of loss, I want to prove my charm and reach out into a new life. But she looks away, too cool to chat, and the wretched attempt falls dead between us.

California, 1994–1997

Home IV: Guesthouse in Sausalito

Sausalito has an excellent climate, an excellent location. If you can live anywhere and have neither roots nor purpose, you might choose to live here.

The town is nestled just across the Golden Gate Bridge from San Francisco, at the bottom of steep hills rising up from the vast lagoon that is San Francisco Bay. After you cross the bridge, coming home from the city, you immediately turn right off the hectic Route 101 and wind down a pretty country lane toward the Sausalito shore, nestled between major earthquake faults. You can't help but speed down the hill, like a wolf descending on the fold. Looking up from the water-lapped shore road, you see houses clinging cleverly to the hillsides above, each leaning out for a glimpse of water, a thousand proofs of a peculiar human yearning. At night, the yellow lights of the houses running up the hill make a pyramid, a Christmas tree of lights. This is how I describe it to Zoe in my mind, making magic of it through her eyes, as I drive home, ill and headed for bed, crashed from teaching a late night class.

I describe everything to Zoe in my head these days. I became used to this in Santa Fe, storing up daily thoughts and observations for her. When something seems strange and marvelous to me, it no longer seems sufficiently strange and marvelous until I've told it to Zoe, and had her marvel at it too. It's the little things—the interesting dog, the sensation of a drive-through car wash, the peculiar man with his parrot—that let me live my American life freshly, as a child again. But now she's little interested in telephone descriptions of a place where she has never lived, and may believe she never will.

I imagined this place, twenty years ago, before I ever knew it, sitting then in a scoured African village, on the edge of the Sahara, tired peasants squatting around me, starving, but willing to answer my questions, human life brought low. I wondered then who it was at the far distant end of life's balance, tipped up high, suffering least, receiving most, and I imagined a glistening place like this in California: white people, clean streets, lapping water, a nervous preoccupation with tiny pleasures and slight advantages, a guiltless bright blue sky.

The little wealth of that village in the north of Nigeria was all spent and the historic grandeur of their Fulani kingdom was long ago eclipsed. Gone too was the richness of their gardens and the feasts remembered by the old. The British, the World Bank, their own government had each come and each had left them poorer. All that was increased was the work of survival, and their fidelity to Allah.

We were all Marxists then, idealistic young Europeans. It made sense in explaining all this, before Marxism became something unfashionable, to be put aside for the sake of career advancement. We understood the way the low end of the balance was connected to the high, the way the power of the rich in rich places made sure the poor in poor places stayed poor. We knew that if there was this starving village, there must also be this gleaming town.

Sausalito, Marin County, California: a rich place in a rich state, in the richest country in the world. My new home. I'm here because on the earlier visit with Mary, we came here looking for good schools for Zoe. We wanted to benefit from this wealth. And when I finally arrive on my own, spent, and with a whole unknown city to search, I look here, so as not to be overwhelmed. I find and take this tiny guesthouse before the search exhausts me. It's modern, glassy, one room with a sleeping loft, my fourth and smallest American home. Also the most expensive. Just temporary, I tell myself, until things are sorted out with Mary. My lesbian landladies in the big house require no lease and say a dog will be OK, which clinches it.

Down the hill from my new home, between the water and the land, is a fringe of a thousand masts, white boats laced prettily into marinas. Most remain unsailed for month after month, the owners with insufficient time, or with an excess of competing pleasures, to make use of them. The yachts are marginal acquisitions for their owners, something relatively inexpensive at a few hundred thousand dollars each, to be kept in reserve, just in case they're ever wanted. By my calculation, I've worked in several countries with gross national products lower than the value of the neglected boats moored here. Most could sail across an ocean, but few will leave the bay. When the cold mist sweeps in from the sea past the Golden Gate Bridge, it turns right for San Francisco and leaves Sausalito, to the left, in the sun. How the perched houses will tumble when the earthquake comes.

Work

In New Mexico, I had long lain in my quiet bed. The snows had come and gone through three winters. And through my bedroom window I had countless times watched the ice form on the bush outside and melt again as the day advanced. The woodpeckers had arrived, pecked at the house, and then moved on with the seasons. I'd learned the lumps and rocks of the dirt track to our house, the sight of them and the feel of them underfoot. I'd bought Zoe toys for three birthdays and three Christmases, and more toys between. Mary had brought morning tea to my bed one thousand times, and held my hand with her rough-tender one as many. Arthur had in this time grown into the oversized black nose and the big dog bark he'd always had, progress noted daily for his fifteen months. Each night I'd warmed the bed for Mary, waiting for her and her easy conformation. I'd felt better in this quietude.

A shock, then, to open my office door in San Francisco:

"Sorry I'm late. You know, I was having sex with this boy and it was going so great I didn't want to stop. You know how it is. Hey, honesty is the best policy, right?"

"I'm so pleased you've arrived. Wheeze. All the other faculty are prejudiced against me. Wheeze. It's this mask. Wheeze. They won't accept me into the program. Wheeze. You can give me permission to audit your classes if you want. Wheeze. It's in here, in the rules.

Look! Wheeze. I brought my manuscript. Wheeze. You're not prejudiced against science fiction are you? Wheeze."

"Not transvestite, transgendered!"

"I'm working on another career too, in case writing doesn't work out at first. Well, actually I'm working on two. I can't decide which is my real strength. I'm working up an act as a stand-up comic, but I'm also taking evening classes to be a dominatrix."

"I mean, what should I do? How, as an African American man, can I be in the same program as someone who writes about African Americans like that? What right does a white boy have to think he can portray black characters? It's offensive to me. It's a hostile environment. I want to know your position on that. I'm taking legal advice."

"You see, if you can sign off on my credits from this college I went to in Oregon to count toward my degree, and take over the incomplete I got from the professor who left last year, and if you could petition the administration for me to have this course counted as a language requirement, then, if you take me on for directed writing using the work I've already done on my manuscript, then I can be out of here at the end of the semester and get to join my husband in Florida."

"Don't forget the Chicks with Dicks show tonight. Ben Mendel in playwriting is in it. You know him, the one who wears a tutu to work. Yes, the professor."

"Don't forget the sexual harassment meeting. We're being sued again."

"It's about this guy who's really into drugs, who kills someone but can't remember doing it. Then it's like this big philosophical question about whether he's really guilty or not. They say, write what you know, right?"

"Lunch? I can't remember the last time I went for lunch. I just bring a salad from home and eat it while I'm seeing students. You'll get used to it."

"You're all narrow-minded bigots! Everyone here. I know I'm a good writer. I know it. I'm too good for any of you fucks to appreciate. None of you here has written anything that matters. Fuck you! I don't need you." [Sound of a slamming door.]

And, "I'm sorry about shouting at you last week. Really sorry. Sometimes I get a bit excited. Writing's hard. You know that. If you'd be my mentor, I'd be very grateful."

"I've been looking forward to you coming for over a year. I love the English sensibility. I lived there for a year. In London. I think my writing's very English, very subtle. It's not the sort of writing most people are doing here. Not much sex and drugs. I can't tell you how grateful I am that you're here."

"It's about my first lesbian experience."

"It's about my first lesbian experience."

"It's about my first lesbian experience."

"Hey, we've been short of men around here, man. I've got scared to take my work to any of the women professors. Or the fag guys. Man, I tell you, we're a dying species out here. You write about hitting a woman or banging her while she's tied up or something and you're fucked around here, man."

"Hi! Can I come in? I'm one of your students, but I'm also a realtor. Have you found a residence yet?"

"Frankly, I don't need these courses. I did my tech start-up a few years back and cashed in, and I'm set. I've got a lawyer in New York negotiating a book contract right now, and a promotional tie-in. I just need the degree to get out of here. All I need to know from you is whether you're going to help me or get in my way."

"So, we've been wondering. Are you gay?"

"It's hot in here. Mind if I take this off. Oops . . . guess I should have worn a bra."

"I need to say that I find that book cover on your shelf offensive. Women feel vulnerable seeing an unclothed body in your office. I mean, I know it's art but it shows an insensitivity toward the way women have been historically portrayed and abused. If you refuse to remove it, I'll have to take it up with the administration."

"I'm . . . mmm . . . doing this article for a San Francisco magazine. On sex clubs. For my day job. You know, like Plato's Retreat. Wondered if you'd like to do the research with me. Hey, just an idea."

In Spokane the people I knew seemed eager to move on, set on leaving the pain of home behind. In New Mexico they seemed keen to stay put, settlers in a foreign land. Here, my first impression is that there is no interest in either moving or settling, when being unsettled in San Francisco is so sexy. The energy is daunting.

Long Division of Body and Soul I: Strippers

There is an etiquette, she tells the class, in elaboration of her story.

If a regular customer passes her in the street, the man should not ignore her but should offer a polite hello. He also should not ogle her, as if she was still a sex object. He should never approach her as a friend and never, never try to pick her up and make a date.

The polite hello is good, and she also likes the faint smile of complicity behind the back of a wife, who would have no idea of what her husband really got up to. There is satisfaction in this: disrespecting hypocrisy. But he should always understand that the transaction is complete and show respect for the off-duty sex worker, who is often, in real life, like her, a clever graduate student with leftist politics and a kind nature.

Nothing real has happened. There is no connection to endure. It is the market.

There's something about love here in California that is making me feel uncomfortable and old. The traditional tests of sound behavior in conscience and code are being left far behind. Instead there is cheerfulness, brave daring, with an agreed price trumping all moral complication. No sin. Body and soul have become divided, and gone their separate ways.

The transaction described in today's writing workshop manuscript is this: She lies on a floor surrounded by booths with windows and letterboxes. When men push money through the letterboxes she crawls over to them, spreads her legs, pulls back her labia and lets them peer into the pink inside, while—if inclined—the men masturbate. The men are quite busy, what with delivering the money through the letterbox with one hand and masturbating with the other. When the money stops she closes her legs and crawls toward another booth. The older Chinese men like her especially and have this way of pushing their hands apart, like swimming breaststroke, to encourage her to spread herself more wide.

There is nothing demeaning in this, she asserts. On the contrary, it is empowering. She is a woman who possesses something so powerful that men will pay for the right to look at it. And she gets a kick out of this, the showing. Many of her colleagues, often students too, are lesbians in their lives and their performances are doubly an act, but she says she likes men. It's just unconnected with her life. It's just the market.

Her male classmate, housemate and workmate, working for the same employer, is less fortunate. His job is to clean up the booths after the masturbators, which pays less and is no fun—other than spending the workday not noticing naked women. The two are not involved with each other and currently neither has a lover.

There is etiquette here too. He should never refer admiringly to one of her performances, which might hint that he was sexually, rather than professionally, engaged. And although he sees her naked during work hours, they respect each other's modesty at home. They do not walk around half-dressed or enter rooms unannounced. It's a constrained liberation.

Something odd has happened to sex in San Francisco. It is everywhere, but everywhere mediated. My office door must remain open at all times to eliminate the possibility of sexual harassment, or the appearance of it, or the false accusation of it. I must affect, while poring over the manuscript of a pretty student in her calculated clothing, to be unaffected by her story of satori through drug-enhanced multiple penetration.

Looking admiringly in any situation is judged offensive, as is flirting, chatting-up, pursuing, importuning, seducing—all the cheesy old freelance ways of getting together, all ambiguous, uncontrolled, unregulated, unpriced, and actionable. Filling the gap are endless pages of advertisements seeking partners, with lists of requirements in appearance and sexual predilection as specific and detailed as the options lists for cars. Or, for the impatient heterosexual man there are lap dancers, massage parlors, escorts, and phone sex, with arrangements similarly available for other sexualities. These transactions are currently judged good, bold, unambiguous, the women in control, freed from harassment and properly rewarded. Market good; human frailty bad.

Sex seems to be everywhere, though it's not for me. I have only the shadow of desire for it. I want the warmth of it in love, and would like the proof that comes with lovemaking of a persisting manliness, but I do not have the energy. Women sense I do not have the energy and instinctively dismiss friendliness as fraud.

Africa was the opposite of California. Here everything personal is made into a market transaction, while there every market transaction was made personal. You can cross national borders in Africa with a smile, a handshake and time taken for a chat—or a greeting in the right language, or the name of someone in the official's home village. I never paid bribes. The women there who lived by sex insisted on dancing with men before choosing them and then transformed customers into boyfriends, paid not with money but with shopping trips and favors to their relatives, drawing them into the web of their lives. A post office clerk once refused to sell me stamps until he had made me a friend to his satisfaction. A bank was opened up for me after hours because the manager came from the same tribe as my girlfriend.

In San Francisco a young Nigerian woman is brought to me one day because I've lived in her country and might help her. She's in her midtwenties, pretty, and planning to stay illegally in America. A boyfriend brought her over for a visit and either he dumped her on arrival or she dumped him. It's not clear. In any case she's determined to make it on her own. When I ask how she will earn a living, she says, "I will strip!" and laughs. She is proud of her brazenness and this grasp of practical necessity.

I tell her what I have learned about employment opportunities from my students' writings, and that the strippers work is to open their legs and expose themselves to men. She replies, "No! You lie! I could not do that. Not even for a husband." She believes that taking her clothes off for an audience should be enough. It seems a lot.

I also tell her about lap dancing, how the girls sit on men's laps and are paid by the minute while they wriggle around to make men come. She wrinkles her pretty nose in disgust. "In their clothes? Why they not fuck?"

I tell her, too, that at twenty-four she might already be considered a late starter with all the competition from young students paying their tuition fees. And I'm wondering about the child she tells me she's left behind with her family, and the toll it might have taken on her body, a slackness of breast unimportant in Africa, but significant in this place of commonplace physical perfection. They like them young, I say. "You lie!" she says again, but with less force. She is crestfallen. She does not like me. I try to make her feel better by telling her that she is exceptionally pretty and I may be wrong to discourage her, but it is too late. I do not see her again or learn what happens to her.

Lost Love I

They are a family portrait when I arrive back in Santa Fe on the airport bus. Mary has arranged it so, to remind me. There she is, standing, Zoe on one side of her and Arthur on the other. Zoe and Arthur fly at me, not a reservation in them. Mary hangs back, in her way. I've been away a month.

In a month, Mary's phone talk has become more distant, Zoe's more insistent. The days in Sausalito are juddering past, composed only of lying down and working, crazed by nightfall every night. No room for a new life. The phone calls home have been everything and they have been faltering. I've flown back to Santa Fe to mend things. It was a toss-up between the damage of travel and the damage of loss.

I walk Arthur a little way up the dirt road in the way I always did, taking in the magic of revisiting the recently familiar. To my surprise the neighbor from the trailer next door, the one whose daughter adored me and who has exiled her alcoholic husband to a shed, comes out to greet me. She never does this; she does not much like Mary, whose reserve she takes for snobbery. "Well, it's good to see *you* back here," she says with pointed emphasis. I reply, "Thank you. It's good to see you too." Later, I bring up the puzzling emphasis with Mary, wondering if she had been complaining about my absence. Mary looks away, shrugs. "I don't know what she meant."

I go to the kitchen cupboard, ruffling through the packets of food. "Do we have any hot chocolate?" I look up to see Mary standing behind me, uncharacteristically agitated, shifting from foot to foot. "Don't do that! I hate it," she says, then she gives an odd, pained laugh, embarrassed at herself.

It takes me a moment. It was the "we." And my easy assumption that I am at home. I understand. To Mary I have gone, not just gone away, a treacherous abandonment like her father's, the one she said was of no consequence. I say, "I'm sorry," and gently close the cupboard door.

On the final evening Mary comes to me where I am watching TV, Zoe on my lap. "I found these in the dryer," she says. "Your socks." I look. "They're not mine," I say. She looks at them, then looks at them sharply, then pulls them to her heart, then turns and leaves.

The next morning, while I am packing, she stands by me and brings up a subject that I had dismissed from my mind, offering, "They could have been several people's socks. Don and his family were here. And Carl stopped over on his way from Montana to Mexico, as usual."
I reply, "Of course," nodding agreeably, keeping my attention on my bag, intent on discounting to myself the unthinkable implication of this. Mary has never been one for explanations.

The Things They Say

You're *looking* well."
"But you *look* well."
"You don't *look* ill."

"I'm tired too. Everyone's tired."

"I used to have something like that, but I got over it by strength of mind."

"I think people who are sick for a long time want to be sick."

"Have you tried X? You can't say you've seriously tried to get better until you've tried X."

"What sort of illness is this? If you're sick, you either get better or you die."

"Oh, you mean yuppie flu!"

"ME disease? You mean you're sick of yourself?"

"It's time you got over it. Everyone's bored with it."

"I wish I had chronic fatigue syndrome. Then I could claim disability."

"I'd never get something like that. I look after myself."

"Yeah, the *Wall Street Journal* had an article about that. They said it was a scam."

"That's a woman's illness, isn't it?"
"That's a rich people's illness, isn't it?"
"That's a white people's illness, isn't it?"
"That's just a fad, isn't it?"

"If you were really ill you wouldn't be able to drive/walk/fly/write/make love, et cetera."

"Just snap out of it."

"I know you're really ill, but I think you exaggerate it when it's useful to you."

"I heard it's a sort of AIDS. There was a book about it. You probably got AIDS in Africa."

"Tried antidepressants?"

"In the old days we couldn't afford to be ill."

"In the old days when you were ill, you just got over it. Had to."

"Don't you think it's all in your head?"

"It's my turn to be ill."

"Isn't that what the Duchess of Kent/Cher/Keith Jarrett/Claire Francis/Laura Hillenbrand/Barry Sheene/MichelleAkers/Darwin/Florence Nightingale had? Look what they've done."

"If people help you, it will only make you helpless."

"It won't matter soon, will it? You're getting old anyway."

Doctor XVIII: Care

My hopes for the long-term benefits of the enzyme potentiated desensitization treatment for CFS, based on the book my mother sent me from England, persist after I leave the ambiguous care of Thumper in Santa Fe.

I'm accumulating a pile of newspaper clippings and books championing a wide range of theories and treatments. Apart from those prescribed by my doctors I am currently also submitting myself to a treatment detailed in the London *Daily Express*, which describes the benefits gained from cold water immersion, as advocated by the former world motorcycle champion Barry Sheene, also a sufferer. It's reported that he's feeling better from the shock of it—though in fact he is soon to die of other causes.

My new San Francisco doctor, the specialist who knows and laughs at Thumper, does not do EPD, but if he is against it, he knows better than to say so. He is not against anything. In this respect I am finding that American doctors tend to be exceptionally accommodating. I discover the nearest EPD practitioner is two hundred miles north in the provincial city of Redding, a place completely unlike San Francisco.

The doctor is a sweet woman in her forties. She is soft spoken, wide eyed, and patiently sympathetic. Her hair is short, her dress unpretentious, and she wears no makeup. In her hands I feel genuinely cared for, so that I now wonder at the absence of this feeling with the other doctors. She tries to save me money, and between my bimonthly visits she sends me little notes on scrap paper with treatment ideas or the content of articles she's seen. She lives—apparently alone—in the same house as her practice, which has the feeling of a home, so that I visualize her waking at night with concern for her patients, reaching for their files and scribbling down her thoughts. Her work is not a job; we are on her mind.

The other patients are nearly all female, typically middle-aged and overweight, though the doctor herself is slight. At our first long interview she wears an odd white jumpsuit, vaguely clinical, that seems uncomfortably tight, the fastenings straining. She brings my attention to this by gripping them with her spare hand while scribbling notes. I have the impression that she has come straight from her solitary bed in the next room and dressed without thinking.

If a good heart, commitment and responsible doctoring were all that was required, this doctor would cure me. Five years after I last see her I receive a handwritten note telling me of a case similar to mine that has turned out to be mercury poisoning and that I might have myself tested. I'm still on her mind. As it turns out my mercury and lead levels are very high, but of no consequence to my illness.

A Treatment:
Enzyme Potentiated Desensitization

Take every two months until better, worse, worn out, or broke.

It is quite deliciously inconvenient.

Two weeks in advance of treatment: Stop all other drugs and medications, including aspirin.

Give up—in turn and according to a specific timetable—coffee, tea (including herbal), soft drinks, allergic foods, dental treatment, toothpaste, newspapers and new magazines, computers, printers, copiers, detergents, deodorants, anything chemical, housecleaning, proximity to animals, exhaust fumes, exercise, heat, and sex.

Oh, and avoid any stress.

One week in advance: Take a massive dose of nystatin to kill the fungi and yeasts that live in your gut. Supplement with precise doses of Tagamet, Diflucan, bismuth subcitrate, acidophilus, magnesium, zinc, Rocaltrol, vitamin C, flax oil, and folic acid.

You've got to admit this is serious medicine. They couldn't make this up. This treatment is like an extra full-time job.

Try not to be too dizzy teaching while you are drugged and undernourished. Spend more time immersed in cold water.

One day in advance: Adopt a stone age diet. Eat only boiled lamb and sweet potatoes with sea salt and no seasoning. Drink only purified water. Rest as much as your work allows in preparation for your big effort on the day of treatment.

Begin avoidance of Arthur—three days late—by relocating him into kind landladies' house. Arthur is hurt and does not agree that his proximity could make you ill.

Day of treatment: Start out five hours before the appointment. Drive two hundred miles through avocado, almond and olive tree country until you reach the end of it. Stop in the middle of the journey to rest at an olive farm. Order purified water at their cafe.

Treatment: Receive an injection of allergens combined with the beta glucuronidase enzyme. Lie down in one of the Lazy-Boy recliners in the doctor's dimly lit house for two hours to be monitored. Say bye-bye and thank you to nice doctor.

After treatment: Drive one hundred miles. Stop at a state park to lie down comatose by a stream for at least an hour. Eat the stone-age soup you brought with you in a thermos. Drive the other hundred miles. Arrive home distressed. Lie down on the rug until you are able to climb the steps to bed.

Two days after treatment: Be incapable, because of the effort of driving four hundred miles two days before. Teach a horrific class during which head falls onto desk and will not come up. You never miss a class. A student stands to complain forcefully that you are not publicly praising him energetically enough for his work. You apologize.

Two years after commencement of treatment: Recognize that it has had no noticeable effect other than the relapses caused by driving four hundred miles under the influence of strong medicine and a restricted diet.

Lost Love II

She says, three and a half months after I have left New Mexico, she says, after one of the silences that are so much part of her—that inward distrust of words—she says into my aching brain, as I lie flat on the Sausalito couch, receiver balanced across my face, she says, "I can see another way."

I wait.

"An alternative way. An alternative future."

"For us?"

Again, a long silence.

"It isn't like when I left my husband. I'm not angry. You'll always be in Zoe's life, I think."

"There's someone else?"

"In a sense."

"You're involved with someone else?" The heart pounds, the pulse slows, the brain spins, the color drains, the stomach drops. I observe all this event.

"Not exactly. But I can see an alternative future. It's for you too."

She has decided, of course. I know Mary. After all, she left another man for me. Her decisions are private and definite, not subject to debate. If the man is as yet undecided, she will decide him.

There is, as it turns out, an old colleague, a professor living in a more southern part of California, a man with a good job in her own field and a home for them to go to. A fit man, with surplus socks.

My brain, bruised by the effort of work far beyond its ability to properly function, tries to be reasonable and measured. It tries to assemble a recollection of what reasonable and measured might be like. My body, alarmed by its multiple malfunctions, is telling my brain that there is grave danger of losing the help of love, and it should do its best to save us. Do not reproach. Do not reproach. If you reproach, she will put down the phone. She's done it before. Absorb. Manage. Be reasonable. Be loving. She is our only help.

I hear something snap. It just lets go. Like that! It breaks, and breaks free in me, spinning freely without traction, disengaged, to where it will continue to spin for years, spewing useless thoughts in the basements of my mind: useless anger, useless replaying of loss and hurt, useless self-justification. The articulation between sense and feeling has just broken. "Unhinged" comes to mind, an old term suddenly gaining precise meaning. The mental buoyancy that has kept hope afloat since childhood, through any reverse, has suddenly failed, the effort no longer sustainable.

"I can't talk, Mary. I'll call tomorrow. Just one thing."
A reluctant, "Yes?"
"I still want Arthur."
A pause. "Yes, we'll let you have Arthur."

Arthur on the Headland

There's this place I'd like to show you, Zoe. Not many people know about it. It's where I go with Arthur every day on my way to work. You go toward the city but instead of crossing the Golden Gate Bridge—you've seen pictures of that—you go down under it, along some winding lanes that go through an empty area owned by the army. Then there's a dirt track which leads to a little grassy headland overlooking the sea. It's not very high. You'd be able to climb it easily. And from the top you can see San Francisco and Alcatraz Island, where there used to be the prison, and Angel Island, where I went with your mom in a sailing boat once. There are lots of seals around there and they come close to you, barking. They look and sound like a sort of dog but Arthur has not shown much interest in them since the first time. I threw them some of his dog biscuits and they ignored them, which I'm sure offended him. Sometimes I bark back at the seals which gets him a bit excited but he probably just thinks I've gone mad.

Every day Arthur runs straight up to the top of the little headland when I let him out of the car. During the week there's hardly ever anyone else there. Then, when he reaches the very highest point he squats to do his pooh, and it looks funny somehow because when he's hunched over like that his shape against the sky is the same as the shape of the headland. And he always faces the same way, across the bay toward the city. There he is straining, with his eyes crossed, staring out at the most expensive view in America. I think he's making a joke.

He gave me a big fright the other day. He decided he wanted to go off exploring. I think he knew I was going to cut his walk short because I was late for class, and he decided to extend it himself. He ran off through the bushes up to a higher part of the cliff on the other side of a little cove from where I was standing. Then he walked out along this narrow ridge which was less than six inches wide and ended high above sheer drops to rocks and surf on every side. You know how he's loved to climb ever since your mom took him out searching for dinosaurs in the mountains when he was a puppy. But there he was at the very end of this little ridge, his four feet all crammed together so he couldn't go forward and couldn't go back. He looked across the cove at me—he wasn't very far away as a bird flies—with that look he gives when he's done something stupid, like eating tar or getting sprayed by a skunk. You know the one: I've been a silly dog; please do something; I know you can.

I can't always keep up with Arthur these days and I didn't know what to do. I started to follow his path up the hill but I couldn't go fast. And I wondered what I would do when I got to the cliff edge. I'd need a rope to get down to where he was and there was no rope and no one to help. I was terrified that he would fall and die. I did not dare to even call out to him in case it made him lose his balance. When I got to the edge he was still looking at me with that helpless look and I decided that I would have to go down and try to help him, even though I couldn't see how. He's over a hundred pounds now, nearly twice your size. But I couldn't just leave Arthur, could I? It just seemed that life would not be worth living without him. He's my best friend here.

I think he must have seen the worried look on my face, because you know what he did? He took his eyes off me, them stood right up on his hind legs, his front paws in the air over the sheer drop, and he did a little pirouette—you know, the spin that ballet dancers do—so that when his front legs came down again they fell back onto the narrow ridge he'd come along. Then he pushed himself up—he's really strong now—and scrambled back to me, slipping and sliding, arriving wagging and full of himself, leaning against me the way he does when he wants to make sure I still love him, asking for me to put him back on his leash. He's an amazing dog. I hope we'll find a way for you to see him again soon.

Waitress: Zuleika

The only women I notice these days, in my daze, are waitresses: young American waitresses who cross the radar of my weak attention. Unpromising of course, but with my heart gone and much of my mind too, they look right. In age, they tend to fall between Mary and Zoe, the woman and the child in one. I'm into my second year in California. Mary has long demurred from talking, passing my calls straight on to Zoe, who has too many dads to please. It must be a year since I last saw Zoe, when I went to collect Arthur from New Mexico. She was staying with her father; Arthur had been abandoned to strangers at our old house; Mary was elsewhere with her new lover. In presence the waitresses are simple: a bit of kindness, a bit of a talk, a bit of flirting, all paid for. Love lite. I aspire to no more, and these are the only women I see other than the off-limits students, since I move from sitting in the classroom to lying flat in my bed with only stops for meals and outings for Arthur in between.

American waitresses are the best in the world: friendly, hard working, witty, democratic, and often strikingly athletic. Waitress today; dancer, writer, artist, lawyer, actor tomorrow. Or maybe wife or lover. Or maybe none of these. So far, I have not progressed, but, exceptionally, I invite Zuleika, who is neither particularly friendly nor hardworking, to dinner, and she agrees.

"Zuleika, is that your real name?" I ask some weeks after she first serves me.

"Hmm? Oh, a friend of my father started calling me that when I was around thirteen and I guess I liked it. So it's my real name now. I guess." She shrugs, tired of it.
"I see. It's in a book, you know. A young woman who a whole city of Englishmen die for."
"No kidding. I didn't know that. I thought it was after some sort of European ballet dancer or something. Russian, maybe."

She works in a breakfast joint, a place always crowded, and famous among the rich new inhabitants of Sausalito for the authenticity of its arty, salty characters—who are now reduced by the same newcomers to prized scarcity. Her beauty is of the precarious kind: lovely features that are almost too large and too fine. I tell her she reminds me of Julia Roberts, though taller, of course, and she replies, "Yeah, I get that a lot."

Both she and Julia have magnificent smiles which, when fully lit, stop just shy of dental overexposure. But Zuleika, at six feet three, also has legs so long that they stop only just shy of freakishness. She's a mountain to climb, four or five inches taller than me when I am standing, which was rarely. If you act like a fit man, you'll be a fit man, goes my unexamined theory.

What makes Zuleika most desirable is the way the breakfast customers crave her attention. Marin is full of aging men with ruined lives, and money in the bank, who feel entitled to a young woman on both counts. They fight with pathetic valor for her smile, but rarely win it. During working hours Zuleika, who is penniless and stalled in life, is empress of the Sausalito boulevardiers.

The cafe is convenient for me, and to save the effort of shopping and cooking, I've taken to eating there during its slack hours. I've been careful not to push myself on Zuleika, pocketing my desperation for company. I've been there a score of times before I ask her name. I'm careful not to leer. Sometimes she talks to me, sometimes not. Sometimes she has snappish bad moods that last for days, making the cafe owner despair. When she begins to confide,

I discover that she is a dancer not currently dancing, and a student not currently studying. She has a bad boyfriend, a musician from Jamaica; she's scared of him and wants to separate, but how can she when he's living in her apartment? The black moods come from this, and other eroding disputes and tussles, resentments, fears and jealousies, an unexpected paranoia behind her queenliness. She's rangy and gorgeous and should bestride the globe but is riddled with a rot of worry, which was why her smile, so close to Julia Roberts's, does not quite glow with stardom.

We meet twice for coffee at another cafe. People know her. She's something rare in Sausalito: second generation. Her parents were there in its arty, bohemian days—sandwiched between its fishing days and its prime real estate days—but they later vaporized, leaving their daughter behind, arty and lost. The graybeards held over from her father's time still treasure her, and in her company, I have the only hints of what it might be like to belong in this place.

When she agrees to dinner, full of anxiety that the boyfriend might spot and punish her, I tell her she should wear high heels, that she shouldn't be shy of that. "Don't be afraid of your height," I say, "flaunt it." At six feet seven, she'll have eight inches over me. I am lying in the gutter but looking at the stars.

Dinner means evening, a time of day I rarely function. Climbing Mount Zuleika will require base camps and rest stops, with all resources brought to bear on the final assault of the summit. I will, ideally, be able to make bright conversation, withstand the attention of strangers in a public place, exhibit cool authority, and, in the unlikely case of exceptional enthusiasm, be able to make love. I start working on it three days in advance with cold water hydrotherapy and extra bed rest. I've not told her I'm ill. She's a young woman without vacant space for the problems of others.

I am dreaming. I am dreaming of a potent self who can win a young woman everyone wants, who is a public match for a towering beauty, who can demonstrate that he requires no sympathy by consorting with a needy young woman incapable of it, and who, at the end of the day, can still deliver. That is, I am entertaining still, in some deep place, the notion that this illness might, after all, be in my mind, or an expression of a broken heart, and might, after all, be banished by an affirming act of life, most potently an act involving youth and vigor. It's a popular view.

Zuleika is dressed up, in stilettos, and stunning. "Wait a minute," she says. "My friend is coming to join us for appetizers. She's a student in your department. You don't mind do you?"

The friend, less favored, is there, I believe, in case I am dangerous. It does not matter that Zuleika could flatten me with a casual swat of her long arms. Men in Marin do terrible things to women. You can't trust anyone. We are in a land of pretenders, scammers, and suspect beneficiaries of life insurance. The friend proves to be deeply skeptical of me. She is the lead counsel for the protection of Zuleika. "Why," she prosecutes, "if you say you teach in my department, haven't I heard of you?" What are they imagining? I explain that it might be that she is an undergraduate and I teach only graduate students. She looks unconvinced, looks at Zuleika. Who is this man really?

This is draining. The cold water hydrotherapy has braced me to cope with the conversation of one woman at best, predicated on the notion that it would be intimate, calm and short. Now my charm is being called upon to disarm two, at least one of whom, with lowering brows, is attached to the idea that I am a criminal imposter. Not to mention the trouble she might stir up back at the university. The evening is in the balance. I roll back my measure for success to maybe a peck on the cheek, or the promise of a second meeting. The friend shows no sign of leaving after appetizers.

I take an inventory. I'm still OK. Upright in my seat. Muscles not singing too shrilly. Heartbeat not too conspicuous. Mental grasp acceptable. Then the stir-fry blurs. I lean back but the food refuses to return to focus. I understand that I am about to crash.

After five years all the evidence is that nothing can halt the progress of a crash after the first wobble, when the canary muscles of the eyes give out. I try to ignore this. I always try to ignore this. My voice is bubbling up from underwater now, reaching my dinner partners slowly: "What are you planning to study, Zuleika, when you return to school?"

The two women look perplexed by the question, frowning. Did I say something quite different from what I thought I said? My back is tensed now because my body wants to slide from the seat onto the floor and I barely have the strength to resist it. I wait for the ripples of conversation to be reflected back to my shore but nothing comes. I lean back casually, arm hooked over the chair-back for support, affecting a sardonic smile. I think, OK, go for louche.

They are very far away now. But I know what they are thinking: He did not have a drop to drink, so it must be drugs. They know about drugs, and drug-taking criminal impostors. Graying men preying. The plain friend is whispering in Zuleika's ear. Saying what? "Let's get out of here?" Or, "Let's take this guy for everything he's got?" I reach out for my glass of sparkling water but my spatial judgment is off now and I flip it over. "Ugh!" they exclaim, the stream heading toward them. People are looking. These are not the envious looks I'd hoped for.

"Dessert?" I ask brightly. Zuleika's friend is looking at me horrified, while Zuleika's expression, I'm relieved to see, is closer to puzzlement. But I can no longer remember Zuleika's name. I'm trying very hard to remember her name.

"No," says Zuleika. "We should go now." Then, unconvincingly, "Can we pay something?"

"Yes," I reply firmly. Since I can no longer generate new thoughts I'm stuck with the one I had before I crashed: that the friend is an imposition and that I shouldn't have to pay for her. Also I am now helpless and vulnerable so that my emergency brain is hyperalert for those taking advantage of me. I'm in the cranky, paranoid phase. "Something for her," I clarify.

They look at each other with a sort of fear, then scrape around in their purses, whispering. They come up with a total of eight dollars toward the hundred. "Thank you," I say, taking it.

Zuleika stands, and stands, and stands. She's way up there, catching the eye of all the diners in just the way I imagined. Here's the procession: first, Zuleika making rapid progress across the floor with queenly, high-heeled strides, eyes front; second, her standard-sized friend, red faced and scuttling; third, me, foot dragging, shoulder slumping, contorted face, bloodless and disturbing to behold—the Quasimodo of Marin—hobbling toward the door in a vain attempt to sustain the claim that I'm with her, the tall, young, beautiful one who's dashing for the exit.

Something; I want something. Zuleika has stopped in the street while her friend has moved on ahead, urging her to follow. I catch up with her but cannot speak. "We'll walk," she says, not unkindly. "My sister lives nearby." My eyes are looking at her chin. It's a fine chin, with a childlike delicacy. "Good night," I say and go for a chaste embrace. Anything. Her body bends a little at its middle and her chin strikes me sharply on my forehead.

I stand, watching her go. A hundred yards away—safe—she turns, sees me still there and flashes the big smile, makes the big wave. I turn toward my car. Arthur, detecting my approach, stands from where he was dozing and pushes his big head far out of the window. It vibrates slightly in evidence of a tail wagging at his other end. I put my head against his and embrace his muscled neck, leaning into him and his doggy smell. "Hello, my good boy. Thanks for waiting. We saw them off, eh?"

I do not go back to Zuleika's cafe for a while, and when I do, she is not there. "No Zuleika these days?" I ask casually of the owner. He shakes his head frowning, as if to say, No thanks, no more Zuleika.

Doctor XIX: Theater Doctor

This is the one who knows the one in Santa Fe, and knows his nickname is Thumper, and that he is a joke.

A year and a half after being admitted onto the waiting list to see Doctor XIX, and a year after I first actually see him—by reputation the best specialist in the Bay Area—and in submission to whose wisdom I am, among other treatments, now injecting my own buttocks daily with vitamin B12 and vials of glutinous human immunoglobulin requiring a painfully large bore of needle, a year into all that, I receive a circular:

"As many of you will know," it begins, "I have long had an interest in the theater."

I am not among the many who know.

What I know is that this is a tall, handsome man in his late thirties, gay, dark haired, and of grave demeanor, whose shoes are hand-stitched by Italians, and whose shirts are perfect and, like his ties, silk. He looks expensive. I've trusted him for his reputation and for the silence that precedes his economical pronouncements. These he invariably delivers standing, either too pressed for time to sit or afraid to crease his clothes. Only his recollection of Thumper causes a slight smile. He knows the literature; he's an expert. The expert.

The circular continues: "I have been fortunate enough to be accepted into the graduate program for theater directors of the University of X in New York. Those of you familiar with the theatrical world will appreciate that this is an opportunity not to be passed up. I will therefore be closing my practice as of May 1st. In the remaining two months there will be, as you may imagine, many demands on my time and it is a cause of some sadness that I will be unable to consult with as many of you as I would like. I regret any inconvenience these new circumstances may cause you, but I am sure you will understand the urgency with which I need to act, and will wish me well in my new life."

I do not wish him well. I am depending on him. I am doing a number of odd and painful things to myself at his recommendation, and though they do not appear to be working, I am concerned that he should see them through to their conclusion. I call his office and am told he will be unable to see me. And, no, there will not be another doctor to replace him.

I am annoyed, but do not trust my annoyance, given the tendency of CFS to drive me into unreasonable crankiness. And my outrage is further hobbled by an encroaching sense that all my ethical instincts are unsuited to California. I call the colleague from the university whose connections won me my original appointment. "Isn't it great," she gushes, "that he has the courage to change his life like that and follow his bliss. With everything he has to lose."

I tend to think it is selfish, unprofessional and precipitate, but I do not say this. Somehow I sense that this view will count me as mean spirited and boorish by local standards. Unreliability here is just a facet of prized spontaneity. It's an expression of personal freedom fully lived, and lived most frequently, I've noticed, in the failure of people to keep appointments on the slightest pretexts. Perhaps I too should learn to bend and claim the moment, adapting to the values and beliefs of my new home. "Yes," I say. "I suppose so. It's great."

The last I hear from my California doctor is on the radio a year or two later. He's talking on National Public Radio from somewhere on the East Coast. There's his good voice and that clear, careful way of speaking that makes you feel such relief in having finally found an expert to trust. It's not as a theater director he is speaking but as a doctor, a world expert on CFS in fact, making a case for its seriousness, the epidemic size of the problem, and the complicated nature of its pathology.

Following which, presumably, he puts down the phone and returns to his theater class.

Dinosaurs

What did I learn about dinosaurs?

That Mary had a secret one in the Rocky Mountains waiting for her, like a secret lover, for when she finished digging up the Seismosaurus, an animal so big its footsteps were like earthquakes.

I learned that two hundred million years ago is a reasonable stab at dinosaur time. Two hundred million. Same planet; different world.

Toward the end, small, poorly evolved mammals scampered between the dinosaurs' legs, with no clue that the future was theirs.

Dinosaur experts are concerned by questions such as what made the dinosaurs go extinct, when they were doing so well. Whether it was a surprise like a big meteorite, or a volcano, or whether it was a long fade. The question has a tingle; next time it will be us.

Or such questions as whether fossils are bone or stone.

I learned some names—some 'sauruses—but never as many as Zoe knew, or all the other children. I've forgotten them now: bad memory. Children love the days of dinosaurs and liked Mary for living in them. They could be the small mammals scurrying between the dinosaurs' legs, freed from everything the adults have done.

Two hundred million years. The entire span of humanity repeated two thousand times. Or ten million human generations, if we had been around that long. Time enough for a hundred thousand Christianities arranged end to end.

This was still recent for Mary, who loved rocks even more than she loved fossils.

I learned that dinosaur experts are very concerned about other dinosaur experts, guard their secrets, and are contemptuous of the glib, handsome ones who appear on TV and get big grants. They dislike them enough to make up bad scientist jokes about them. All scientist jokes are bad.

Like many dinosaurs, Mary was cold blooded and only warm when the outside temperature was hot. Otherwise she shivered and pressed up against me in bed. Her movements were deliberate and efficient, too slow to warm her. I thought of it as a sort of depression in which it was the temperature that was depressed. She liked Africa, hot deserts, and Southern California, where she came from. No trace of her Irish genes, except in the fairness of her skin. The Irish feel cold less than anyone.

Immediately after I left for San Francisco, Mary went to a geology conference in Chicago, unearthed an old lover there, and glided from me like a glacier.

Sadly, she moved away, deliberately, without a backward glance, a klutzy, long-necked sauropod, a heedless, harmless herbivore, for whom looking back would be a great to-do, and all the damage of its path, incidental.

Zoe calls me for two more years after Mary moves to California with her new lover, and we have bright conversations, each one revealing my slackening grip—through eight, nine, ten—on her tastes and habits, her playthings, her favorite TV, the names of her friends.

I learn that dinosaurs leave eternal traces where they die, polished stones that they'd kept in their gut to grind up food. They are like jewels and Mary gave me some. Pretty, smooth, too common to be valuable. I remember now: gastroliths; that's what they're called, gastroliths.

Long Division of Body and Soul II: Toni

The relationship I can manage in California is the one with Toni. I pay for it.

She starts off well, by saving me. The man she saves me from—Rick, according to his tag—is a staff member at a health club in San Francisco. I've been booked in to learn stretching exercises that might ease the pains in my muscles and joints, and he, chest thrown out, is loudly denying my right to instruction. Feeble in body and mind, and taken aback by the unexpected hostility, I am having difficulty articulating a response. Toni—according to her tag—bounces over and slips between us, her chest to my chest, taking my arm, and taking me away. To Rick, she says, "Don't worry, I'll take care of it." And to me, at a safe distance, "Don't worry, he's a jerk."

She stands too close and touches too much, laughing all the time, while she twists and turns my body. She asks personal questions and renders personal answers without any obvious filter of prudence or reserve. She seems full of a reckless joy, all American in manner, some Asian in her looks, late thirties, fit, compact and curvy. My spirits are lifting. "I married an old man," she volunteers. "He doesn't take much notice of me."
"Foolish man," I reply.
"I've an idea," she says. "I've just finished my massage therapy certification. Want to be my first customer? Cheap massage."
"Sure." I'm new to massage therapy, but eager to follow the light.

"OK, keep it quiet. I'm not supposed to find private clients here. Can you come to my house?"

Its intimacy surprises me, that this can be so readily bought. Again, California has me off-balance. In a nervous place, where a glance can cause suspicion and a backfiring car in Sausalito has recently provoked a police stakeout for highway snipers, I am lying naked in a stranger's living room, the house secluded and otherwise empty, surrounded by flowers and soft music, a sheet placed across me in notional decency. Toni is massaging me, smiling, pulling the pain and tension from me.

She catches me; the massage becomes my weekly hour of bliss.

We talk easily, all openness and indiscretion. Sometimes she brushes against me in ways not quite correct, or I passingly rest my hand on her in ways not quite correct. She smiles, laughs. Touch, talk, mischief, something like affection. All arguably within the bounds. Toward the middle of the sessions I turn over to lie quietly on my stomach, while Toni kneads me with such skill that my muscles and brain unclench and I feel the brush of much needed sleep. Which is exactly when, to signal completion, she kisses me softly on the top of my head and leaves me alone to recover. Such restoration for thirty-five dollars. So modest a price. Bless her.

Outside, waiting in her kitchen when I emerge dressed, Toni has artfully arranged on the table between us a tall glass of water, glistening, and some special treat from a chi-chi confectioner, ginger, or chocolate-covered cherries, and she glows with pleasure at my pleasure when I sit to join her.

She has treats for Arthur too, leftover pork chops and prime rib such as he has never tasted, so that when, at the time for my departure, I release him from where he has been waiting in the pickup, he bolts to Toni with a mad enthusiasm that ends with his nose docked in her crotch. Her unembarrassed response to this disgraceful behavior is to stand braced on the front step, her arms thrown wide, and call out to him, "Come and get it!" She is rude life.

Over the months I learn everything about Toni. She was born in California to an Irish American father and a Korean mother. There was a brief, early and forgotten marriage, and a child from that, now grown. Then there were a number of rich married lovers supporting her during a decade-long gesture toward being an artist. She has never been to college. The last lover bought her a gift shop, soon sold, to mark his abandonment—for which she was grateful, his judgment correct, she now acknowledges, that her talent was more for decoration than for art. Then, forestalling the incipient need to introduce herself to regular work, she met her present husband, who was a businessman then in his sixties against her thirty-two. Six years ago now. "He saved me," she says in explanation, giving me a sad, pleading look. This new career is really her first. "I'm looking for some independence," she says. "And a way of connecting. I have a gift for making people happy."

In turn, I tell Toni all about my life, and in endless detail about the loss of Mary and Zoe, to which she listens patiently and professionally. I allow that my restlessness may have contributed to the problem, which she translates back to me as a healthy openness to life. "The thing I miss most," I tell her, "is being a sort of father. If my health doesn't improve I may never be in a position to have children of my own."

They are wealthy, but they are also bankrupt. She explains this to me patiently, as to an infant. They ran up big bills and then engineered the bankruptcy to avoid them. "Everyone does it. We're borrowing again now to rebuild our credit. That's why we have new cars. It's what you have to do. You can't build your credit unless you borrow."

Toni is my great sustainer who I fear to offend. I am becoming attached to her in spite of the unsuitability. But I feel I have to say something before my moral foundations are swept away before her. "Isn't that a bit dishonest, Toni? I mean, other people are paying for your bills, probably people with less money." Toni stops working on me. She looks shocked, uncomprehending, offended. I tell her about my family in London, how we didn't have much money but were always scrupulously careful, never buying anything we had not saved for. I tell her how, to this day, I gain a sense of virtue from buying my car for cash not credit. Toni's face remains clouded from absorbing all this, but she finally brightens and finds a revivifying dismissal. "Well, hello!" she says. "You're in California now."

Sometime later, while she is extracting pain from me and anointing me with life, Toni tells me of a new endeavor. "We're suing the health club. For sexual harassment. My husband's lawyer's on it. We're going after Rick. He's always grabbing and hugging me." I agree that Rick is disagreeable and give her the approval she is courting. I do not say at this time what I am thinking: that nobody touches people more readily or riskily than Toni.

Not many weeks after, she tells me that they've settled their case. The health club has paid up, and its manager fired. "I'm thinking, Italian vacation," she says.

"Why the manager?"

"Because he's responsible for the club's financial loss," she explains.

"Not Rick?"

"No, he's still there. They can't fire him. It would be admitting fault."

I do not say what I think, that this all seems unfair. I say, "So, I suppose you're looking for a new place to work."

Toni looks surprised. "No, I'm still working there."

Nothing personal, it seems.

I am at the health club and see Rick and Toni cantering down the steps together in front of me, as I make my slow progress in their wake. They have not seen me. Toni puts her arm around Rick's waist in her spontaneous way, pulls him close to her, then squeezes his bottom before releasing him to go her separate way.

I feel, in California, like a moral cart horse in a field of frisky lambs.

"Look!" Toni instructs, after I am settled on the table. She lifts her skirt above her head. "New underwear!" There are ethical standards for massage therapists, but Toni just flows around them. She explains: "I feel safe with you."

When her massage of my hand produces an erection—new evidence of the body's mysterious connections—Toni lifts the sheet and looks below it. "Nice penis," she says, and gives it a joshing nudge.

Or she guides my hand to rest on her breast, offering me a brief, luscious reintroduction to womanhood while continuing with her professional task. I sigh at the feel of it, the memory, distant now, of how it was when I had a lover to touch, and was loved.

This suits me well enough, this sexiness without the exhaustion of sex, an intimacy concentrated into ninety minutes a week and contracted with a thirty-five-dollar payment. Toni suits me, now.

Toni sits close to me, my leg trapped between hers, my knee lodged beneath her skirt. Her thighs are remarkably strong. It's very pleasant, really, the warmth. Toni always touches; she is touching the waiter while we order, warming him too. Her husband is out of town and she's invited me to her favorite restaurant for an early dinner, our first time together outside of her massage studio. Once again I am lamenting the loss of Mary and Zoe, my own wretched part in it and the agony of lost fatherhood, and once again Toni is sympathetic. We fall into silence, each with our own thoughts.

In an unfamiliar, girlish voice, Toni breaks the silence to say, "I'll have your baby."

"What?" I'm taken aback. Our relationship is chaste. California is full of sex, but I'm not actually having any.

She repeats herself: "I'll have your baby. You said you want to be a father. I'm still young enough."

I look at her. She looks serious. It's true I've longed to have a child. "Toni, how would that work? You're married and I'm sick."
"I like you," she says in the same plaintive little voice, which somehow signals our entry into an alternative reality. She looks uncharacteristically earnest and her thighs have tightened. It occurs to me that I've never really taken Toni seriously, or imagined that she could take me seriously, and that those massages, long talks and treats have been more than was due for my thirty-five dollars. "It could work," she says.

Her husband, she explains, is not happy. "He's really miserable. He has a heart condition, and he's hardly interested in anything these days. Not even in me. It's like I told you, we haven't had sex in years. I'm all he has. I'm the only one who makes his life worth living. I'm the one who has to be there to make sure he takes his medicines. But it's hard, never getting anything back. I've been doing this for four years now, since his first heart attack. He doesn't have any friends. I can't live just for him. Even though I've got lots of energy, I'm tired of it now. I want my own life. But I could never leave him."
"Right," I say, "I understand," thinking that I do. "I can see you're stuck."
Toni looks at me for a moment and divines a need for elaboration. She plunges on, her voice still plaintive. "I can't leave him. If I leave him, I know he'll die of misery. And I wouldn't inherit or get life insurance. I can't be poor, again. I just can't. We'd need the money for us to be OK. You and me and baby."
I'm puzzled, speechless. Toni holds my look. In recognition of her pain, my part in it, and my inability to comprehend, I give her my hand. Out of habit she begins to massage the palm in the familiar, arousing way.

"I'm nearly forty now," Toni continues. "I've never felt sexier in my life. He's over seventy. He's had his life. It would be the best thing for him. I like you. I could look after you. Make you happy."

I think I may understand. Toni seems to be proposing that she helps her husband die, so we can be together and live a comfortable life. I'm smiling, not talking. I'm taking in this idea and doing nothing with it. I'm a very long way from home. And this is Toni who I am fond of, and grateful to. Toni, who is life. My mind, turning sluggish with the day and its progressive loss of neural plasticity, is struggling to bend to the proposal. Perhaps this is OK, in California? My difficulties could be overcome at a stroke: love, money, care, parenthood.

Once, an acquaintance in London told me he was working on a highly corrupt and illegal weapons deal, and I pretended not to hear rather than own this dangerous knowledge. It seemed best. Now I am not hearing Toni. I'm squeezing her hand as if to communicate that I sympathize with the pain she finds in her present life, and that any specifics she may have mentioned consequent to this pain are irrelevant to me.

"Why shouldn't you share my dream?" she persists. "Like in your friend's book."
I'm taken out of the moment by this, then realize what she means. The memoir, written by a colleague, is the only book Toni has read during the time I've known her. She was unable to progress with mine, but she has read this one—a best seller—several times. In it the author divorces well and details her triumphant new life in an Italian villa with a new lover, complete with recipes. Toni has set it prominently on the bookshelf otherwise occupied by Martha Stewart magazines.

I still say nothing. I am making a show of perplexed thinking.
"I've talked to people," Toni says. "It's what women do here. Younger wives." Then after more silence, there is the tiny voice again: "I'll have your baby."

At last, I say, "I'm sorry things are difficult for you." And, "By the way, Toni, I think you're wonderful and your husband's very lucky to have you. I wish you could have my baby."

In the parking lot, before I leave, I kiss her on the mouth for the first and only time. I'm feeling inexplicably OK. I'm kissing a potential murderess, but, hello, this is California.

The next week, I turn up for my massage as usual. I need it. In between I've crashed into a relapse. Toni gives me a long, soft, reproachful look but says nothing. She starts to work on me, then takes a breath and sets the tone. "Something's puzzling me," she says. "I've got this client. He's really unattractive to look at—fat, hairy—and he doesn't have a good personality either, but every time I give him a massage, I get wet. He makes me wetter than anyone, yet I don't find him the least bit attractive. How do you explain that?"

Nuts

I am beginning to act strangely. I'm still teaching, inventing new courses and receiving good evaluations from the students, but I exist within an increasing level of distress. My brain, asked to do so much, so publicly, with so little of it functioning, has reached a new pitch of resistance.

Neither lying flat for hours, nor immersion in shockingly cold water, nor the twenty medicines that comprise a medical Manhattan on my kitchen counter are providing sufficient help. I have no remaining social life and no sexual feeling. I look yearningly at women but I fear that however favorable the circumstance and availing they might prove to be, I would be unable to act. I can no longer reach out into the world. My true place is alone, and in hiding.

First, I cut off the beard that I've had since I was twenty. I do it roughly without shaving cream so that the shape of the beard is recorded in raw pink skin. I look like a baby, pink and round, or perhaps more like Winston Churchill in his dotage. Out of sight beneath the beard, I've aged. My jowls have dropped.

Next, I take to photographing myself daily. I've never liked taking photographs and so I have almost no record of my life in Africa, Asia, or London, but now I work out how to set my camera for self-portraits. I have no idea why I am doing this. I take one every day. I'm always sitting on the couch, always unsmiling. This man looks dead; perhaps the photographs are to disprove it.

My brain has become the object of my dispassionate consideration. I see it as simply a damaged meaty organ that will no longer work. Its condition interests me. The right cerebral hemisphere has the feeling of being swollen, saturated, inflamed and pressing against the inside of the skull. There are excessive demands on it which, instead of being crisply processed, simply irritate and disappear. On the other hand, the left side of my brain seems to have become inert and shrunken, like a dried walnut. I do not sense any activity over there at all. The electricity and blood have been switched off as if for failure to pay the bills.

Pushing new daily efforts into this failed machine—insisting that it keep ahead of ambitious graduate students during three-hour classes, asking it to also spend part of the day impersonating a woman from Zanzibar—is, if not flogging a dead horse, then flogging a diseased nag with two broken legs and a heart condition. I now understand "the loss of neural plasticity and inability to manufacture new memories," in three-dimensional terms. Pushing new information into my brain is like trying to push toast into an overheated toaster. It pops right back out. But neither is failure acceptable, so I continued to insist. My abused brain, with all its uncompleted tasks, refuses to cool for sleep, and so frets away the nights in the overheated shuffling of its cards.

I can no longer bear it. I am out of optimism, ingenuity, and all resources. If I am not my brain, I don't know what I am. Cornered, I go to the yellow pages and call a number that promises urgent psychotherapeutic help for the desperate. The recorded message of a psychotherapy group practice asks for my name and number and tells me someone will call me back before too long.

But Zoe calls first. I rip myself away from distress. "How's Arthur?" asks Zoe.

I say Arthur is happy. Arthur is always happy. "He's right here," I say. "I'll put the phone by his ear and you can talk to him."

I hear the little telephone sounds of Zoe talking to Arthur, while he lies there puzzled, finally rousing himself to lick the receiver.

“I told him not to chase any more skunks,” says Zoe, when I am back with her.
“He gave you a kiss,” I say, then, “and what are you up to?”
“We’ve got a new cat. A white one. Mom’s called him Chicago.”
“Interesting name. Why did she choose that?”
“I don’t know.”
But I know. Chicago is where she found her new man; this is Mary’s familiar way of evolving a binding family myth. I recognize it. I am full of tears. None escape.
“I miss you,” says Zoe.
“I miss you too, Zoe. You know . . . it’s not so easy for me to see you these days.”
In fact, Mary stopped talking to me when she moved in with her new man and has kept their address secret.
“I know that!” Zoe is sharp, impatient at my stating the obvious, exasperated with the adults.

I get through the call, one of the last from Zoe. She has not seemed to notice anything amiss.

A psychotherapist, Lila, calls next. “Have you had suicidal thoughts?” she asks. “Some,” I admit. She can see me the next day.

Doctor XXI: Not a Medical Doctor

Lying on Lila's couch, I tell her that though I've thought of suicide, I do not believe I will ever actually do it. "It's just that my brain hurts and I want to stop it."

"Have you imagined how you might do it?"

"Suicide?"

Lila nods.

"I've imagined shooting myself. I'd put the gun right here." I pointed to the spot to the right side of my temple where a bullet would go right through the swollen, inflamed part of my brain. Lila winces, as if she's felt the shot. I like her now.

"It's all right," I reassure her. "I don't have a gun." Then I add, "And I wish I didn't live in a place where I can get one."

She's about my age, lives in the less expensive Oakland on the East Bay, and commutes to her practice in a modest Japanese car, which is all I learn of her life. She is very strict with time, the way I've learned New York psychiatrists are from Woody Allen films. I also understand for the first time the difference between psychiatrists and psychotherapists, and that she is the latter because she has a PhD and not a medical degree. I see her weekly, then at her suggestion, twice weekly, then back to weekly.

In spite of my excellent health insurance, I am paying for Lila myself. Someone has told me that I should keep psychotherapists off my university record.

I tell Lila that I've seen only one psychotherapist before, briefly, years ago back in London after one of my many breakups with my girlfriend there. She had quickly declared me whole and healthy and, after a judicious six-month delay, made herself available for a relationship. I'm proud of this story, which I've told before and which portrays me as sane, attractive, and transgressive. The affair was brief, I explain, because this other therapist, once relieved of her enigmatic professional silence, proved to be a self-involved chatterbox. Lila clucks her disapproval. Of the therapist, not me.

Her hair is shortish with a some gray strands, her body tastefully and comprehensively clothed in long skirts. The face is pleasant, without its details ever fully lodging in my memory. Lila succeeds in being an attractive person before being an attractive woman. I believe she is good, and nice. She muddles up her billing, which makes me like her more, her mind being in the right place. I think she might care, but is careful never to display it.

Mostly she has little to do. When I arrive at her office, I generally collapse, stretching out on her couch which is too short for this purpose, so that my legs are hooked over the armrest. I close my eyes and wait for my thumping heart and crackpot brain to quieten. I can rest better with her in the room than I can on my own. I would come here just to lie down. Blinds shield the windows. Lila waits quietly.

When I talk, I talk too much about past loves, the long one in England, the artist in Spokane, and Mary in America—as if the solution to everything can be found there, and in some future love. Restless pondering. We talk about my health too and my job; she had practical proposals for reducing my workload and learning about any benefits to which I might be entitled. I explain that I had pretended to be fit when I took the job and fear to reveal that I am not. She probes gently at my fear of public failure and my terror of ostracism. We talk about childhood bullying at school.

At her prodding I ask the university for, and receive, a reduced workload—along with reduced pay. I discover that this arrangement is not unusual, not even unexpected. Many of the healthy faculty find the work overwhelming and have discovered ways to save themselves. I hardly see my colleagues and so do not know this.

I've heard of transference and wonder if, with all this talk of women, I am disappointing Lila by failing to fall for her. It feels impolite. I do not even have a sexual dream to share, or any dream. I am too shy to tell her of my concern for her feelings. Instead we talk in general about my habit of taking on the responsibility for making hurt women feel loved, and the recoil of resentment that I feel at this burden, and how all this comes from a childhood spent salving my mother's hurts, which, of course, came from her childhood. It all makes sense.

It takes Lila to point out, six months later, that though I am just as sick with CFS, I am no longer imagining suicide.

Long Division of Body and Soul III: Robin

Robin is rich and she is kind to me. We are kind to each other. She's my first real friend in Marin County. She goes to Russia, for the opera. To Italy, for the opera. To Santa Fe, for the opera. To France for the food. Owns a boat and expensive cars. Owns a view of San Francisco Bay as fine as Arthur's. Is divorced. Is athletic. Is lonely, and dissatisfied with it. Is not naturally beautiful, but is working on it. Believes in perfectibility. Now, when I'm too ill to go out, she delivers chicken soup to me in a Porsche.

We have a limited conspiracy of the damaged: my health, her wealth.

I first meet Robin in a cafe on the day she is going into the hospital for investigatory surgery. She's nervous and, because nervous, talkative. It turns out that the only people she can ask to go with her to the hospital, and drive her home while she is groggy, are people she pays, which is causing her some distress. I know about lonely hospital visits and offer to keep her company.

She weighs me up carefully, as if I might already have researched her bank accounts and engineered this meeting. But she believes in artists, that they are profoundly different and illogical, and so while her surgical investigation is underway, I read student manuscripts with my feet up in a waiting room, surrounded by people whose loved ones may be dying. It turns out that Robin does not have cancer.

She finds it hard to spend her money. Sometimes even the best is not sufficiently expensive. She goes to classes to learn how to give away money without being harassed by the recipients. She wants to buy friends but does not want a friend who can be bought. She wants to be wanted. She thinks there is something hidden in art that she might need. Meaning, perhaps.

She is the person furthest away from the villagers I once worked with in Africa. I like her but can't love her. She is energetic and kind and laughs readily. Unlike the villagers, what to do with her life is a problematic issue. Unexpectedly, the richest person I've met here is also the nicest.

If you are wealthy and single, this is who you pay in Marin (incomplete list):

Undocumented Mexicans for the outdoor work
A pool guy, who visits
A personal trainer—you don't have to be alone at the gym
A personal shopper—to find the right style
A fashion consultant—for taste
A massage therapist—to relax
A speech coach—for your public self
A cosmetic surgeon—for your public self
Hair stylist, manicurist, pedicurist, beautician, etc.
A house cleaner—Nigerian (part-time catalog model)
A restaurant guy to plan your meals and have them delivered
An interior decorator—to arrange your house
A feng shui expert—to rearrange it
Art consultant, antiques consultant
Travel consultant
A dog trainer
A dog walker
A dog sitter

A dog
Two financial advisers—because you can't trust just one
A personal lawyer—kept very busy
Ski instructor, music teacher, language teacher, etc.
Car guy
A psychotherapist—because you need a friend
A relationship counselor—in case you have one
Doctors, dentists, alternative health practitioners
A security consultant—to keep it all inside
Closet organizer—to keep it all straight
A Korean launderer
Introducers—so you can meet useful people
Sex partners—saves time and trouble
A personal manager to manage all these, except possibly the last.

It's a lot to worry about.

It is the long division of body and soul
Life sliced thinner
The invisible hand making progress
Cutting deals
The general is made specific
The personal made commodity
The unsellable sold
The unpriced priced
Each transaction brought to market, taxed and added to the GNP
To count as progress.

I think of this lying in bed in my sleeping loft, waiting for the sound of Robin's Porsche. There are more days now when I can barely get up. I think of her sadness and how she can't find a road in life that will lead her to be fully human. I realize for the first time that my family had been virtuoso generalists, when I just thought of us as engaged in the obvious and necessary.

We cut our own nails—on Mondays for luck.
Dad soled and heeled our shoes

And taught me how
He painted the house inside and out, hung the wallpaper
And taught me how.
He maintained and mended our bicycles
We chose our own house decorations,
Which was unfortunate in the case of the bamboo and rosebud wallpaper
Mum knitted new clothes, darned old ones
Made handkerchiefs out of old bedsheets
We grew our vegetables on an allotment and fruits in the back garden
Mum bottled the fruit, made jams and marmalade
And laid down Christmas puddings years in advance
She did laundry in a tub and hung it out to dry on Mondays
Like all the other women
For pedicure Dad scraped off the hard skin with an old potato peeler
After his weekly bath, after walking a hundred miles on factory floors
We shared the shopping, the cleaning, the bad cooking
We never hired a plumber, electrician, or carpenter, never hired anyone
Dad did it
Grew grass and flowers where there were no fruits and vegetables
Never paid to exercise
You must be joking
I massaged my mother's ankles when they swelled from queuing
Lit coal fires in our grate for heating
And the boiler once a week for baths
Read books from the free public library
Went to the free doctors and dentists
Lawyers were for wills
For therapy, we complained to people in the street
Or stayed unhappy
Stayed ugly and awkward, if we were
Threw away nothing
Our garden shed was built from scrap

They worked for wages too
Both of them
They shot low for happiness.

The market barely laid a hand on us
We were halfway from peasants and halfway to Sausalito
All this is still in me
Which is perhaps why I cannot love Robin
Here she comes
Cheerful
With a Tupperware container of soup big enough for a week.

It's Over, Boy

This is how the last day goes:

Four A.M.

I'm fed up with my brain. In spite of its exhaustion it's been up all night, standing guard, alert against the defenselessness of sleep.

Four fifteen A.M.

Turn on National Public Radio in the hope that it will fill my head with something other than my own productions. I'm in luck. The BBC, which plays at night, has voices instead of the usual music. Music is useless for distraction. Even better, they are comforting English voices. They are acting J. B. Priestley's *Time and the Conways*, a play in which the meaning of time is divertingly considered. I recall Priestley's philosophical Arizona book, *Midnight on the Desert*, in which he compares time to the slices of a loaf of bread.

Five A.M.

The BBC gives way to national news and a bumbling local announcer. Mind-numbingly, he is describing the day's school dinner menu for the San Francisco area, a regular feature. It does not sound healthy. On the East Coast it's eight, and in London one in the afternoon. In Tokyo the stock market has already closed and there's bad news for my savings again. I attempt a quick calculation, trying to prove to myself that if I stopped working I would be able to survive. I persuade myself that the necessary 50 percent per annum return on my savings is not an unreasonable expectation.

Seven a.m.

I move. Up to this time my only initiative has been to reach one hand six inches to the radio. Otherwise I have been entirely still, locked into energy-saver mode.

I topple my legs off the bed, and by a clever exploitation of gravity use this momentum to tip my body upright, so that I am sitting on the edge of the mattress. The effort is about the same as was once required to lift my personal best in a London gym.

At the bottom of the steps down from the sleeping loft, Arthur, a hundred pounds of fit fur, stretches and articulates a long growly-yawn of morning greeting. I reply in kind. It's our little interspecies joke.

I brace myself for the effort of climbing down the steps by promising myself two reliable satisfactions: tea and the cartoon on the *Far Side* calendar.

In the bathroom I stare at myself in the mirror. I'm not really there.

Seven fifteen a.m.

Back in bed with the tea. I pull myself forward to see the sliver of Richardson's Bay that is visible. The water is flat, the street lights on the opposite bank are serenely reflected, the floating homes sit just as they did yesterday. Peaceful. I've assumed violent storms and nighttime disasters.

It is not good news this early in the day that my brain is bloated, my muscles are tingling, and that every joint of my skeleton is a locus of pain. I have a pile of manuscripts to absorb and master before teaching a three-hour class at seven in the evening.

I tell myself to relax and give myself another hour of absolute immobility.

EIGHT FIFTEEN A.M.

Up. Eat muesli. Take medicines and supplements, about twenty. Give myself two injections in my right buttock, which has become very sore. My left hand is inept, so I can't do the left buttock.

NINE A.M.

Send Arthur out to relieve himself on the brambled hill behind the house. He does not like this trick because he thinks, rightly, that it's instead of a proper walk. I can't manage the walk. I'm fairly confident that he will not run off chasing the raccoons because I have not yet fed him breakfast. In two minutes he's back, nose against the glass door. I feed him.

NINE FIFTEEN A.M.

Yoga. It's supposed to energize you, so I've been trying it. I sit on the rug, stretch my arms up and breathe deeply. Arthur lies down next to me and also stretches. Comedian. The energy is supposed to rise up from my groin to my head and then sort of vaporize as pure spirit. Apparently there is no energy in my groin to begin with. I stand. I'm dizzy.

Ten a.m.

Time for serious work. If the manuscripts are to be read and thoughtful commentaries prepared, it will have to be done early in the day when my brain is at its best. At its best today, it feels like oatmeal with a knife in it.

I lie stretched out on the couch with the first manuscript resting on my chest. Immediately I start thinking about Mary and Zoe.

Eleven a.m.

Time has passed. I recalculate the day to assure myself that I still have time to do my work and maintain the minimal fifty-fifty ratio of horizontal work to horizontal rest. It does not work out, but I press on, skipping sentences and grabbing at judgments with the bit of my mind that is available. I like to work with a safety margin so that I can feel that even my worst work will be good enough. I doubt I'm reaching good enough today.

Three p.m.

I've written something on each of three manuscripts, and I am trying to convince myself that this will do. I'm spent. Building myself up for the effort of the class at seven will take all the remaining time.

It does not cross my mind that I could call in sick. If I started doing that, there would be no end to it.

I dress, pack my briefcase and my swimming bag, bundle them and Arthur into the truck.

Four p.m.

Drive to outdoor pool, change, swim for ten minutes. The main point of this is not exercise—I practice a breaststroke of humiliating slowness and stop a lot. The point is that the pool is cold. It quiets the noise in my muscles, numbs the blood away from the surface into more useful circulation, and shocks the nervous system into a sort of frightened life. The moment when I topple into the cold water is not one of unpleasant shock but of welcome relief that all the pains are for a moment trumped by one big sensation.

Back in the changing room I take an even colder shower. My neighbor gets a splash of it and exclaims, "Whoa, you're brave!"

Five p.m.

At last Arthur gets a proper run. We go to the usual headland on our way to the city. He races off to pooh on the summit. I follow slowly. This is my test: if I can still climb the thirty feet or so up, I'm still OK, serviceable, still within the limits. I do it, but my head is spinning.

Six p.m.

I'm at the Chinese restaurant near the university where I always go before class. The idea is to stuff myself with enough carbohydrates to get me through the three-hour class, and to soak it all in stimulating Chinese tea. While I eat, I review the manuscripts and my class preparations, which in the last three hours I have completely forgotten.

Six forty p.m.

I set out for class. This is as good as it gets. I'm medicated, fueled, stimulated by tea, and shocked by cold water. I square my shoulders, pick up my step, and try a smile.

Six forty-five p.m.

I park on the campus. It takes an expensive pass, but parking higher up the hill is essential. I walk toward the humanities building, passing a line of convenient and empty parking spots for the disabled. I have never considered asking for a disabled pass. I am not disabled.

I have to manage twenty yards or so of steep hill. I lean into it and affect a strolling action so that my slowness will appear less odd. I think of mimes walking into imaginary winds. A tall, athletic girl in shorts prances past me. She turns as she goes, alternating running forward and running backward, her step unnecessarily high. She's not in my world.

On the easier downhill stretch I can see myself reflected in the windows of the humanities building. I'm moving as fast as I can, but I'm the slowest person on the path. A middle-aged woman student greets me and I say hello and smile. I remind myself that the students rely on me for support, regard and enthusiasm.

In the building I wait for the elevator, even though the classroom is only one floor up. The elevator is designed to move so slowly that its use will be minimal. While I'm waiting, one of my students lounges against a nearby wall. He's an angry drug user, full of resentment, and normally I would make an effort to jolly him along, but today I ignore him. His manuscript for today includes a detailed account of the violent murder of an Englishman.

Seven P.M.

The sixteen graduate novelists are all present and keenly competitive. They are already successes for having gained entry to this program. I sit down, set for the next three hours. I never stand to teach.

The class is a blur. My eye muscles have given up and I can't read my notes. I am talking. I am there, but not there. There are some spirited contradictions of what I am saying. I see the annoyed faces. Other voices come in to support my case, I think. They are going on without me. There are hurt feelings that I should intervene to salve. No doubt some fine points and breakthrough illuminations are being articulated by this talented bunch and I should capture and highlight them. But they are passing me by. I see faces turned to me in appeal. I try a smile. OK, brain, how about sending me the odd message to explain what's going on. I am becoming very small in my chair, shrunk by embarrassment and an ancient terror of classroom humiliation.

Into the fog, I say, "OK, let's move on," and am surprised at the silence I've produced. "Let's look at Ashley's manuscript now," I say, and there's a frighteningly obedient shuffling of paper. My words sound quite normal to my ear—sort of professional—but they don't have much to do with me, and I've no idea of what to say next. Ashley, bless her, jumps in, "I just want to say something about this before we begin. . . ." And she's off, and they're off.

At the end of it—it has somehow come to an end—there's a huddle around me. I nod approvals, somehow react to questions. Then they have all gone, off to their cars, buses and trams, some to late jobs, some to sleep, some to the bars, parties, the drugs and the sex of their real lives, some home to family. I sit alone in the empty classroom, unable to stand. Maybe it hadn't been so bad; maybe it had just seemed to them as if I was a bit off tonight. I've no idea. I sit there unmoving for half an hour or so, blank, waiting for the little trickle of returning energy to pool itself sufficiently for the journey home.

Ten forty-five p.m.

Pull up at San Francisco's long, cold, deserted ocean beach and let Arthur out. He tears around, splashes knee deep in the surf. I don't follow him tonight. Walking on sand is beyond me. I lie back in the driver's seat, passively allowing the surf, the moon, the stars to imprint themselves on me.

Eleven fifteen p.m.

I'm driving very carefully. I am intent on recognizing that I am unfit to drive. My eyesight, judgment and physical abilities are all off. But I've made it across the Golden Gate Bridge and am dropping down the winding road to the bay. There's no other traffic. I look for the balm that I usually find in this descent toward the water. At the bottom I note a raccoon guiltily nosing his way along the sidewalk by the water's edge.

Eleven thirty p.m.

Home. Arthur heads for his water bowl, drinks a quart, then comes back to me where I'm still standing just inside the door, and presses his wet snout into my hand. I fall to my knees on the rug and then lie down on it. He lies down next to me, and I rest my arms on him, which he tolerates. Our bodies are not very different in size. I look into his deep brown eyes, where it does not seem to matter that mine are unfocused. He accepts this too. Neither of us moves a muscle for some minutes. Then, I say to him: "It's over, boy."

Doctor XXI: Lila Again

"Well, I did it." I'm lying down, my eyes closed. "I told them I couldn't continue."
There's a long silence.
"How do you feel about it?"
"Relieved. Upset. It feels inevitable now."
"Upset, why exactly?"
"Because it feels like the end of everything. The end of the life I came to America to make."
"You don't think you'll go back to work?"
"I don't know. I'm sure I'll feel different when I've had the chance to rest. If I get better, I could go back. But why should that happen? I've tried everything to get better for the last six years. I've never failed at anything important before."
"And how does that feel?"
"I feel like crying. But I never cry."

"I'm worried about what people will think."
"What will they think?"
"That I'm not really ill. That I'm just pretending to be ill to take time off."
"Why would they think that? Your doctors don't have any doubt about you being ill. Why should anyone else?"
"I don't know. I've tried to hide that I was ill. I'm not sure that even those who know believe this is a real illness."
"So, you're anxious that they will disapprove, even though there's no evidence for this. That they'll think you're malingering."

"Yes."
"Maybe because you disapprove yourself? Even though you've done everything you could? You've said that failure is unacceptable."
"Maybe that's it. Maybe I'm projecting my own feelings. It's just that everyone at the university is overworked and tired. There's not much room for sympathy."
"Does it remind you of anything, this anxiety that people might turn on you?"
"You mean, like when I was bullied at school?"
Lila lets this sit in the silence before saying, "Well, perhaps you should wait and see."
"Right," I say. "You're right."

Doctor XXII

Doctor XXII is the one suggested to me by the departing theater doctor, a name pulled out of the air to get me off the phone. They have little in common. He is a bearded, bulky man working in an East Bay clinic with mostly Hispanic patients. No expensive Italian shoes for him, with the trousers breaking just so over them. He's a scruffy family man with a pleasant face, a bit harassed. He's added antiviral drugs to my medicines. Why not?

"I've had to stop working."
"I saw it coming," he says, surprising me.
"I'll need some sort of letter from you. For the university."
"Just jot down what you want me to say and where to send it. What will you do?"
"Rest. Wait and see. I'll be on sick leave for a while."
"Maybe you'll be able to write a bit?"
"Maybe. Eventually. Now I just want to rest."
"My wife's a writer, you know. Fiction. Getting good rejection letters. Any suggestions?"
"There are so many of us. I'd offer to look at her work, but you know . . ."
"I know. Just tell me what you need. I'll back you up."

California Story

She's a tall woman, this colleague, and is standing in the doorway of her home, unsmiling.
"Did you hear?" I say, "I had to stop teaching last week."
"I heard." She's offering nothing.
"I reached my limit," I say.
She takes a breath. "What I heard," she says, "is that the night you stopped teaching you were out partying and bragging about sick leave."

My heart drops to my stomach and stays there. This is—precisely, perfectly—what I feared, and what Lila has encouraged me to think was only my imagining.

Somehow the years of effort, self-blame, loss and loneliness are contained in this moment. Someone has made up a malicious story. They prefer to believe that my illness is fake and that I am fake too. Others hearing it will also believe it. It is the sum of my fears, and I'm taken unexpectedly to a lower place, when I imagined I was already at my lowest place.

"And do you believe that?" I finally ask of this colleague—the one I thought to be the warmest and who I was looking to for understanding. She looks at me appraisingly, her arms folded. She does not want to be taken for a fool. At last, she says, "I don't know."

California has not taken. Not me to it, nor it to me. People will believe this story of me because it makes sense here in a way I do not. It's a way of dealing with me. In a place of triumphant scams, false bankruptcies, insurance frauds, Silicon Valley stock options, and everything for sale, body and soul, they have come up with a story for me that makes sense. It is more credible than the truth. If this colleague believes it, so will everyone, and it will be the story of me in California.

That my worst fear has come true makes my failure perfect. It is of little comfort that some of those retailing the story probably admire the scam and wish they had thought of it first. There is no point in protesting the truth. No one knows me here. It seems I've been a stranger all along, a foreigner moving among them, not fully aware of his foreignness. But they've found a place for me now.

The university is decent and plays it by the book. They do not want to have to replace me, and instead put me on something called Catastrophic Leave for the rest of the year, scrupulously explaining my benefit options should I be unable to return. If they have a skeptical opinion, they know better than to express it. They could be sued.

I write a note of explanation, expressing my regrets and apologizing for any inconvenience, which I mail to all my twenty barely known colleagues. None responds. I'm history now.

Other States, 1997

Leaving

Outside of Bakersfield the road curves east
And rises
So that the skirted town looks low and false
Palm-treed and green in the desert
Overlit and willful.

I'm climbing into the mountains now
The air cleaner and cooler
A sudden access of energy
Speeding me up
As the road becomes more difficult
Searching for the press of life.

I wind down the back window
Of our new Jeep
So Arthur might share all this
His head
Similar in size to mine
Reaching forward into the wind
Until his canine nose
Is alongside my human one
His outside the glass
Mine inside
His attention to what is essential
To his doggy brain
As intent as mine is
To the requirement of the road.

Up to now it's been all wrong
The flyblown interstate
Through Central Valley
The smash of fat mutant insects
Survivors of pesticides
The late-model tag-team cars
Heading south
Suspended between money and money
San Francisco to LA
Air conditioned
Musicked
Floating higher than the limit
They have been wrong.

The stinking stockyards of condemned cattle
Were wrong
As were the slogans of angry farmers
And the damned Denny's restaurant
With its dazed unhappy staff
And the dead flat farm road going east
So clouded by eroded dust
That daytime traffic came at me as yellow lights.

All this was wrong
And there is little to commend my present course
To make it right.

I'm on Catastrophic Leave
And leaving
Yet
This road's new emptiness
And its curves
Its rise
My speed
The leaving behind and below
The fresh evening air
The sudden natural nature of the hills

These are all welcome
And place upon my brow
The cool and comforting hand
Of an escape
Made good.

To Stop

It could not last, of course, my little burst of energy outside of Bakersfield, just a Roman candle in the night. Now, I'm back to driving the way that has evolved for the West's long empty roads, and my limitations: reclined, limp, eyes defocused to the distance, hands resting in my lap at the bottom of the wheel, breaths taken with a slow deliberation, letting America pass. I'm not expected anywhere at any time. No one knows I'm on the road or that I no longer have a home. After six years of CFS my life in America is down to me and Arthur, a car and gas. We're looking for a place to be.

My driving posture requires little effort, but once established it is hard to relinquish since stopping now becomes more taxing than continuing. Stopping involves standing up, speaking, making decisions. It's easier to keep going, but if I do press on into greater exhaustion, then both continuing and stopping will become equally impossible. Making this mistake in the past, I have finally pulled over and sat frozen at the wheel for hours, waiting for revival. Knowing this, I promise myself that I will take the Tehachapi exit and spend the night at the Cactus Motel, across from the railway, where they are easy about dogs and where I've stayed before, with Mary.

Tehachapi might be a place. We need a place. I've irrevocably given up the guesthouse in Sausalito and packed up my things to ensure there can be no return. A place that suits us now will, I think, require most of all . . . no effort. I can't quite visualize it, but it will be so cheap that money will not matter, and the people will be few and private, with low standards for newcomers. There may also be a secret hope in me that once I have stopped I will not always be alone, because one day I'll discover, or be discovered by, a woman, perhaps a waitress, since this is the only sort of woman I now imagine meeting. I'll lie down and she'll talk to me about the violence in her life that brought her to this place. I don't belong to the universe of happy people, nor do I want to belong. Happy people are tiring, tiresome. The waitress will be pretty underneath her ruin, and will slowly blossom. I'll be kind. An expression comes to me from economics—"low barriers to entry"—said of businesses that require little capital or skill to establish. Low barriers are matched by low rewards. I'm looking for a place with low barriers to entry to lie low, nowhere too small, remote, or humble for consideration. Low rewards would suit me very well.

I have no plan and no great eagerness to arrive. I'm drawn to the desert first. To small towns. A return visit to New Mexico will be hard to resist, since the memory of life with Mary and Zoe is so with me. But I'm in no hurry to meet those memories.

Tehachapi's main street, shallow as a movie set, is one-sided, facing the railway. A couple of motels, a couple of restaurants. The railway looks touchingly mechanical, a holdover from Victorian times, never modernized for sleek high-speed trains, an anachronism suggesting that the cruelty of time has failed to be cruel enough.

I like it that going east from the California coast you climb up to here and that, soon after, the road cascades down again to the Mohave Desert. Tonight, Tehachapi looks cool and beautiful, and apparently not yet fashionable. If I came here, I would come unencumbered, without friends or family or career or health. I would start small and would endure: an inexpensive, quiet life, untroubled by hope. And if the tide rose from the coastal cities, bringing with it artists and cappuccino, I would have, without effort, the authentic status of an early arrival.

I'm stopped next to the office of the shabby motel, sitting in recuperation mode, alive but barely functioning. A human body on standby. The tape of Anthony Trollope's *Barchester Towers* has been playing without my registering it. I need a mist of words to cool me. Now, as a first step toward consciousness, I let it seep in, lending my mind to Trollope in preference to the life outside. The elderly Mr. Harding, who is marked as a good, mild man, looks like he is going to run into trouble when the new bishop arrives to take up the position that should have gone to his son-in-law. Who knows how this tussle will play out? Someone will rise, and in consequence someone else must fall. The zero sum arithmetic of Victorian England is a gorgeous relief after the crazy new math of California.

If I stayed here in Tehachapi, I'd be friends with the Indian owners of the Cactus Motel, who I know from earlier visits to have family in London and East Africa, including Zanzibar. We may know some of the same people. In any case, they would understand that I'm used to Indian ways, easy with Asian extended families, not a stranger really. I'd mention my ex-girlfriend and her family in London, and how close I was to them, and they'd make space for me among the exiles.

The woman from Zanzibar I've been irregularly impersonating for the last five years in my writing came from East Africa and London too, and at the end of the book I've left her here, in Tehachapi, making friends with the Indian owners of a motel as a new life promises. She's on the run, having killed someone. Ridiculously, I'm looking for belonging among new immigrants more strange to America than myself, and insanely, I'm choosing for my model the fictional woman I've invented.

I shake myself into acknowledging the necessity of dealing with the business of renting a room if I want to arrive at a bed. I go to the desk, ring the bell, and lean against the counter, as if I don't have to. There's a sound of noisy eating from behind the screen, a full deck it sounds like, from crying babies to cranky senility.

Human warmth. A teenage son I haven't seen before comes out, chewing, to deal with me. He's modern, hair streaked blond with a trace of the faux cockney accent recently fashionable in London. He moves away, talking on a cell phone while I fill in the card. I'm an interruption, an unwelcome member of the necessary public, but he's easy enough when he returns to swipe my Visa. He gives me the key and I say thanks.

"Right," he says, covering the phone. "Know where the room is? Just down on the left."

"Sure," I say. "I've been here before." But my voice is faint and he's already back to his phone and dinner.

Tehachapi

I'm taking this seriously. I've bought the local paper and over breakfast I intend to consider the situation and divine whether or not Tehachapi might be right for me.

The cafe is next to the motel. On the wall are photos of wind turbines on the hills outside of town—the same ones that I had the woman from Zanzibar admire for their graceful intelligence and quiet company. Other photos are of the Voyager, a light plane that apparently took off from the Mohave to circle the world nonstop, and this street, after it was flattened by an earthquake. Tehachapi's distinction apparently rests on three legs, each depending on geology. Absent from the photo gallery is Tehachapi's other main draw, the women's prison. None of this seems unpromising.

I've been here—what?—five or six times on my way between San Francisco and Santa Fe. That's almost a habit, almost a belonging, a potential first brick in the construction of a life. The elderly waitress, though, gives me no hint of welcome or recognition and instead looks offended by my bloodless order of oatmeal, dry toast and tea. The cafe is empty except for the old boys at the counter joshing the old girls working. Above the grill a mesmerizing old contraption electrically flips over the homemade advertising cards of local businesses every few seconds. Click, flop. Click, flop. A well digger. A realtor. A motel.

OK, snap to it. Clear the mind. Dismiss the past and any thoughts of Mary and Zoe. Today my mind will never be more able than it is now, over breakfast. I have perhaps half an hour of clarity in which to decide whether Tehachapi should be the location of my future life.

I smooth out the local newspaper in front of me. Top headline: "County Buys Property Near Tehachapi Landfill." Not immediately seductive, but it does have a certain small-town authenticity. I flip to the real estate. Not bad for California. A hundred thousand buys a decent house and an acre. Back to the front-page headlines: "Zond Proceeds With Expansion Plans." The Zond Corporation builds those stately wind turbines, so that's good. A little green shoot of economic life. Good.

The next headline, "Tehachapi: What Does It Really Mean?" seems made for me. I want to know. But the author is irresolute. He says the name comes from the native Kawaiisu, and could mean either flat place covered with oaks, or plenty of water and acorns, or windy place, or hard climbing. Meaning dribbles away.

The other front-page headline is "Megan's Law Puts Squeeze on Sex Offenders." Tehachapi has five of them it seems, and though they have served their time, they now must declare themselves and post their addresses for the neighbors. Instead of feeling relieved on behalf of Tehachapi's women and children, my heart goes out to the offenders in their foiled attempts to establish new lives in an out-of-the-way place. I now imagine the Tehachapians to be suspicious and self-righteous, and my own vision of a tolerant acceptance fades. But the offenders are monsters, perhaps? I read on to discover a list of qualifying sex crimes that includes oral sex, sodomy, sex with under-eighteen-year-olds, and indecent exposure, including urinating in public. I'm guilty. Everyone I know in America is guilty. Many on all counts. I feel the chill of illogic.

My time is up, and Tehachapi hasn't taken. Disappointing that. I choose the long route out of town. We pass another, glassier center and outskirts where people are building brash new homes with mountain views and horse farms. These new arrivals are not hiding but conquering. At the town limits I stop near an unofficial rubbish dump to let Arthur relieve himself before the long drive, then—criminally—decide to do the same. "Ready for the road?" I ask, and he offers a joyful dance of assent to whatever it is I've just proposed.

Into the Desert

By Mojave, twenty miles downhill, I'm spent, though it's only 9 a.m. I settle to the straight desert road. First there are fields of mothballed airliners stored where the air is dry and the land has no value. Later there are the long wire fences of shy government installations built back from view, their hidden intentions betrayed only by the warning signs.

My thoughts settle too, now I've lost the energy to elevate them. In the basement of my consciousness, rumbling around like boulders, repeating themselves endlessly and randomly, are blaming thoughts of Mary, whose love did not last.

At the top of my consciousness, constantly replenished, is the soothing sound of *Barchester Towers*, Trollope's blessedly leisurely novel. This stratum of my mind is occupied with ecclesiastical intrigue in Victorian England.

Sandwiched between the Victorian intrigue and the irrational resentment is a thin stratum of actual, present life: vague impressions of scenery, the business of driving, an awareness of Arthur's needs, and sporadic consideration of how I am, where I am, and where I should go next. Absent from this mental geology are the higher functions of plans and planning, for which no resources are available. Not planning takes me through the desert to an old mining town where only a gas station and cafe have survived an earthquake, and to a neat and prosperous little town with many cruising police cars, which only makes sense when I spot the military installation on its outskirts. The former draws me more than the latter, but I don't want the trouble of earthquakes. Mary claimed she liked them for the way deep old geology humbles us.

What about Needles? I rather like the look of Needles. There's a sort of downtown of wide streets and old buildings which is more or less deserted. And there are chaotic outlying areas of modest homes. There's a character to it, though it's hard to define, and I don't try too hard. It looks poor. What do people do here in the hot desert? It seems like a sort of staging post, within the borders of California, but Nevada by conviction.

At the post office three large grizzled men are looking for mail that might be held for them. They have biblical gray beards and tattoos, but judging from their walking staffs, they do not possess the motorcycles that their appearance suggests. Rather, the dust on them and their boots suggest they have walked here, emerging out of the mountains according to a purpose far outside the mainstream. Their spokesman talks to the postal clerk in a quiet voice, patiently insisting on a package that the clerk can't find. Their fearsome bulk and oddness make the clerk panicky, but he can't produce the package, only the repeated use of "sir." Finally, the men look around, confer and withdraw, as if they might have chosen not to.

After a night at a Chinese-owned motel, interrupted by a fight conducted in Spanish, I decide that Needles is an outlaw town where people are incurious about each other because it's too hot to go out. It would be a good place to, say, assemble drug shipments for LA. I like the idea of an outlaw town. Needles might be a place.

Losing It

In Laughlin I've discovered somewhere more immediately devastating than brightly lit supermarkets: the gaming room of a casino. If the delicate state of my body's systems makes me particularly able to detect environments toxic to humans, I seem to have found the most poisonous.

I'm here because the motel on Lake Mohave is closed. Each evening I want to be near water, and I look on the road map for the blue smudges of lakes and rivers. Lake Mohave, being the artificial creation of a dam, is limited in its soothing power, but still preferable to Laughlin with its strip of casinos built along the Colorado River. For a hundred miles Laughlin has been advertising rooms at give-away prices. Mine is sixteen dollars. At the bottom tip of Nevada it's the closest place to Southern California for those desperate to gamble and exists only because of this desperation.

The route from reception to the elevators requires, by design, traversing the gambling floor, inhabited by hundreds, if not thousands, of clanking, dinging, flashing fruit machines, each screaming for attention over the background music. On the perimeter are a few gaming tables, lightly used and apparently only serving to suggest an old-fashioned sophistication à la Monte Carlo. If the slot machines are too demanding, areas for Keno and Bingo are indicated.

I look straight ahead and not at the siren machines, concentrating on moving my feet. The carpet deepens as I progress. My back muscles and jaw are tensing with the effort of walking through carpet, and my brain is urgently trying to bail out sensation faster than it can leak in, while the casino management is set upon the opposite task.

It's the customers who are my undoing. I can't keep from looking at them. They are all old. They're clinging to the machines like monkeys in some awful experiment in which machines have learned to feed directly off life. These people are not rich. These are losers losing. They have tired factory faces. It strikes me as a terrible thing that these noisy machines, guaranteed to beat them, can make it worth their trip.

I've let myself feel, and by the time I reach the elevators I've aged thirty years, now struggling to lift my overnight bag. I'd imagined that a casino hotel would spike the frankness of its exploitation with some flighty, sexy, low-life zest, proving the persistence of vitality. But there seems little prospect here of honest sin, among the spent. My eyes, drawn to the faces, have searched for charm and have found none.

Tonight—and I promise you, Arthur, just for this one short night—Arthur will sleep in the car, in the cool of an underground car park, curled among my things and our smells in his flat domain behind the front seats, a water bowl by his nose, doing the job assigned him—"Guard the car, boy"—with a contented acquiescence that I find almost disappointing.

Eureka

Now, Eureka is a serious contender for my new life. This is my second visit. The first was last week on my way up to Montana, and this one is on my way down again. It's cheap; that's good. And it's an old mining town and I've come to like old mining towns—I've visited them in Arizona, New Mexico, Utah, Colorado, and Nevada—which tend to have some fine brick buildings left behind from boom years and no one much to use them. They are ripe for people like me, who need to live cheaply and have no compelling reason to be anywhere.

My stay in Montana, a state which at first seemed promising in its extent, ended in a town where the only restaurant turned out to be fancy and full of self-conscious people talking about films. I've become used to losers, who don't much care to be looked at and who know better than to look too hard. In this place people were preening and looking and talking, and the meal—for me simply the urgent necessity to refuel—was a horror of scrutiny. I could not hide my unglamorous, failing, slumping, slurring self. After that discomfort, I dropped down south again to the Nevada desert, just obeying gravity.

Eureka is made especially attractive by its advertising, which bills it as the Loneliest Town in America. It is reached by a road billed as the Loneliest Road in America. This seems perfect. The idea of a place of cheerful people busy with their own warmth and sociability has become appalling.

I take my breakfast in the only open restaurant on the main street, a place otherwise occupied today by a group of men in heavy boots and outdoor gear engaged in a strategy session. They have the appearance of prospectors slipped a century out of time. They also act like prospectors in that they glare at me and lower their voices, as if I might jump their claim, or if I overhear them, they will have to shoot me.

Oh, it's enough! I mean I like the loneliness, but I don't need the hostility. I take Arthur for a walk along main street so he can pee on it. "You're conquering America, Arthur," I tell him, "one urination at a time." Unlike me, he has also conquered time, living in the scents of those who preceded him and leaving something of himself behind for those who follow.

Aunt Bee's

I have become, though homeless, a resident of Nevada. The state government is sending me forms to fill in. The reason for this is not my extended wandering around the state but my arranging for my mail to be forwarded to Aunt Bee's mail service, located in Boulder City. Apparently, by doing so I have made myself a resident of Nevada, since—apparently—it is not officially possible to be nowhere. My knowledge of Aunt Bee's comes from the old life in which I owned a boat and subscribed to *Cruising World* magazine. Aunt Bee's has long provided a pre-email era service to cruising yachtsmen by accumulating their mail, then forwarding it to their next port of call when this becomes apparent. Every now and again, I call them and they do the same for me.

Conversation

The east European couple behind the motel desk in this town—Hawthorne, perhaps—are new arrivals and very nervous, chattering to each other in an east European language about the right forms for me to fill in. I try to talk to them—I'm by now experienced in the guest forms for cheap motels—and they stop for a moment to look at me before continuing their conversation with each other. They seem apprehensive, as if they think I might be a criminal or an immigration official, and that they lack the skills to tell the difference. I do have a secret: I am not declaring Arthur, since the sign clearly says that dogs are forbidden. Arthur, with his brilliant cooperation, has learned to leap straight from the back of the Jeep through an open motel door, and to then lie entirely doggo, while I go out for dinner. Witnesses seeing him flash waist-high across their line of vision might not quite believe their eyes.

I've had a conversation, the first for a long time. The chatty lesbian owner of a takeout pizza joint. Maybe Ely. She'd come here for a new life too, from California, she says, with her partner. They've made a go of it, but all the same she's ready to leave. It's not all good for lesbians in Ely, and she isn't sure I would fit in either. Their delivery boy comes in to collect a big order for the brothel just outside town. "He loves going up there," she says.

Vegas

Trollope's all done and I've moved on to the tape of a memoir by the scrupulously austere Annie Ernaux, translated from the French. I'm cruising around Las Vegas, dazed, needing lunch but without the ability to go inside anywhere. I sense that I'm the only person listening to Annie Ernaux in this city. She is writing about her late mother, with a dry, fastidious intelligence that is part literature and part sociology. Few words, each one counting. It's quite extraordinarily lovely and moving. It's marvelous that humans can do this. Outside, a life-size pirates' ship has launched into deafening motion on the sidewalk. There's a volcano erupting down the street. The traffic has come to a stop and pedestrians are crowding around. There's no real barrier between the street outside and the insides of the casinos, except the blast of cold air, nor any barrier between the sidewalk and the road. Annie is describing the pinched, repressed lives of her poverty-stricken parents in northern France, the restraint of her sentences packing extra emotional power. The people crowding around me in leisurewear are soft and candy colored, hungry for expensive pleasures. I met Annie Ernaux once at a reading. She was tall, handsome, frightened, dressed in gray and black. Probably depressed. We're out of the center now, into the empty zone where the new hotels are being built. They are going to be bigger and better fantasies according to the signs, but right now they are just huge steel frames, dusty in the desert sun, the financial calculation showing through, the fleshy fun not yet packed in. How do I get out of here?

Kink in the Road

I'm finding it hard to leave Nevada. Thoughts of New Mexico and the rest of America graze my mind and are deflected. In the past week or two I've made excursions into all the neighboring states—Nevada doesn't have enough roads to fill my time. Some towns in Montana, Idaho, Kansas, Arizona, and Utah have motivated me to buy their newspapers and to seriously consider them, but I've always returned to Nevada. It does seem to be the emptiest. Having proved that I cannot quite imagine myself into any town, I now focus my intentions on finding a particular kink in a road that has stuck in my memory. I can't remember exactly where it is, but I'm sure it's somewhere in Nevada, and the fact that it has achieved a fixed memory gives it special meaning. I can see it quite clearly: a narrow road across the desert intersecting a single rail line at an angle. The kink in the road is so that the actual crossing of the line can be perpendicular. There are a couple of buildings lodged in the kink, old factories or warehouses, and the windows of one of these are entirely occupied by black characters on orange backgrounds—one per window—declaring that apartments are for rent and giving a number to call.

If I can find this place again, I will stay. I haven't thought it through—the local availability of food and drink, for example, has not concerned me—but the quest is giving shape to my days. The kink promises the lowest possible barriers to entry, and it's immediate availability for a new life could not be more clearly marked. It will be a place to rest, where Arthur and I can lie down untroubled. Whatever is making me move on will no longer make me move on, and in the stillness my body and mind will restore themselves. It seems like the perfect nowhere.

And then I am approaching it, and it is exactly as I remember. I'm on a long straight road through flat desert and there is the huddle of buildings at the kink, visible from ten miles distant, the landscape's main event. I slow down to savor my approach. The buildings look more formidable than I remember. Here's the railway line. Slow right down for the first bend in the kink, bump across the tracks, and here is the big building with the Apartments for Rent sign in its windows. Arthur is straining his head out of the car, very interested. The bright orange of the signs has faded a little toward pink, but they are all still there. There is absolutely no one around. Just the beating sun. I stop and efficiently take out my notebook to copy down the number. I look for a pay phone, but of course there isn't one. It only occurs to me now that if every window in the building is taken up with advertising apartments for rent, then no apartment can actually be rented. No one lives here. There is absolutely nothing. But wasn't this what I wanted for my tiny, tiny, new American life, now ambition is over? Arthur is agitated, thinking that since we have stopped, he will be soon be out and about and taking stock of things, but instead I slip the car into gear and drive away from the building, moving very slowly. I don't know what I'm looking for anymore, but it's clear that I'm done with Nevada. Arthur strains his head out the window to look back at the place that he never had a proper chance to master, and which is now shrinking in my rearview mirror.

New Mexico

I've made a date with Mary's ex-husband. The one she left for me. Zoe's dad.

There's only Arizona to cross. I look for water as usual and find Lake Havasu, The Personal Watercraft Capital of America. Without meaning to, I am driving across London Bridge—the exact stones that I first crossed as a child, with my dad, damply cold in a red London bus then, on our way to visit my grandmother in Wimbledon, to a house filled with knickknacks and scented talcum powder. What is it doing here? The far shore is barren, bordering the artificial lake. When we get out of the car, Arthur is spooked by the unnatural landscape and asks to be put back on his leash.

Arriving at Flagstaff, I remember I was first there when I was nineteen, my student summer in America, when I was picked up in the bus station by the sixteen-year-old Hell's Angels girl who took me straight to bed. I had no idea then that her age made this a crime in America. It was a huge and wonderful adventure for a naïve English boy and so exciting that she could not get rid of me. Flagstaff still has a glow. It still feels friendly. Tomorrow I'll be back in New Mexico.

I'm woozy from the waves of feeling that come upon me as the New Mexico roads turn familiar and became populated with tender memories. I slump in the kitchen chair. There's not much for me to do; Mary's ex is a talker, not a listener. He likes to run the show—one of Mary's old complaints. He probably does not know how little Mary has told me about her new life. He may think, because it's what she may have told him, that I left her. He may think that I hardly care at all.

This is where they once lived together, a venerable adobe home in the village's old center. It's a handsome house, shaded by the trees growing in a walled garden. Once the shade must have seem like protection, not shadow. The house feels emptied of a wife and child. He tells me that he recently emptied it more by banishing the cats, along with the dogs. While we talk, Arthur whimpers softly on the porch, his exclusion from a scene of high emotion offending him. He's visited this house before, with Mary and Zoe, and to Arthur nothing quite exceeds the pleasure of return, a world repaired.

When Mary's ex shakes my hand, he leans back, simultaneously moving toward and away, smiling ambiguously, scanning me for something. There always was this, the height, the knowingness, the slight hint of intimidation. The meeting was my idea, but he agreed readily. It suddenly seemed obvious, given the voices in my head. We can't leave it alone.

He's always been decent toward me. The last time I saw Zoe—years ago now—he'd organized it. While she was visiting him and I was visiting New Mexico to pick up Arthur, he had arranged for me to have her for a day. As Zoe had settled into my car, she'd taken time out from being excited to ask—too responsible for nine—whether he might like to join us too. He'd smiled and declined. He'd done this for Zoe more than for me, so she could see me and see that things were all right between the men. We had picnicked, fished, delighted in each other, and I'd delivered her back to him, one dad to another, in defiance of a third.

The third dad, the new one in California, is all right, he now says. He can deal with him. Though he does not much care for the location of their house, expensive though it is, nor the way Zoe is called upon to babysit Mary's new step-grandchild without payment. The new husband is older than I am. It seems he was Mary's doting paleontology professor once, and she'd kept him secreted until it was time to dig him up. It's working out well for her, he thinks. Financial security, family, opportunities in her career. You had to admire her efficiency, never a day without a man. Most of this is news to me and I drink it in, not letting on.

There's no longer much left for him here. His business never amounted to much, he says. You can't make a proper living in New Mexico. This thing, settling in a poor village to make a new life, it doesn't really work. Early in his career he'd worked in advertising, a bright spark, and the village was a reaction to all that, he says, a quest for sanity. It's a good place to have a family, though. Children can run free. The Hispanic women love them. But all that's over now, he thinks.

I think so too. The adobe looks too much like dust. His eyes are red with something—dust, tears, or drink. He'd had a wealthy lover, after Mary, but she wouldn't do. We are left behind. She'd offered so much, and reserved so much. You have her completely and don't have her at all. I agree with him and try to elaborate: She lets you know that she'll be yours completely if you keep to her rules, but the catch is that she keeps the rules secret. He tells me the story about how he and Mary had gone to marriage counseling but she refused to tell the therapist how she felt because it was private. I wonder to myself if that was during the early days of her affair with me, and whether I was the secret she was keeping. It must have been around then that she told me of the tiny, scared person hiding inside her. Somehow we older men knew this and loved the abandoned child in her, with all the risk that came with it.

So he'll up sticks here and sell out. He'll move to California, to be near Zoe. Mary will have to deal with him whether she likes it or not, him being Zoe's father. With me, of course, he points out, it's different. He looks around the artful house and declares it over. We've come to the end of what could be done with the love of Mary and will have to do something without it.

Our parting is warmer than our meeting. I'm sorry, I say, that he's had such a hard time of it. And would he give Zoe my love. I have to get on, I say, on the road. He says that if ever I want to know about Zoe, I can always contact him, though there is the question of his future address, so far unknown.

The Days

The days go like this now, one after the other, not counted. I'm moving east, but not directly. I head north, then south, hanging out for days in anonymous motels when I become too sick to continue. I don't know how long I've been on the road, and I'm reluctant to work it out. Every week or two I use a phone card to check up on my mother in London. I listen to the events of her life spool out, familiar, irritating, comforting, and she asks for few details of mine. All of my life in America has been unimaginable to her, so that my current rootlessness does not seem more strange. There have been three or four calls, I think, so I'm probably into my second month.

It seems necessary for me to collect information on all the middle states, which is nevertheless restricted to the piling up of local newspapers, the checking out of the real estate pages, and occasionally making a jotting in my notebook. I have no vision of a future. Sometimes memory unexpectedly fixes something in me, since the inability to manufacture new memories is neither perfect nor predictable. These memories have no context. Occasionally I jot a sentence into my notebook, little eruptions of the old idea of myself as a writer, a man who makes something out of experience. But my mind is fogged and I speak only to waitresses and motel clerks—just the minimum to get by—so I experience very little, and notice less. I am going through the motions, more afraid of stopping than continuing.

The days have a routine. We get up and find a place for breakfast for me, then a place for Arthur to run. We drive for perhaps four hours. I don't know what to do with myself if I'm not driving; it's become my default state until I am unable. At lunchtime I buy a sandwich, usually from a gas station Subway, and look for water for the midday lie-down, which lasts an hour or two. Then we drive for another few hours before looking for a new place for Arthur to run—watching out for the brown state park signs, but also looking for small towns with civic pride enough to have their own parks. Then a little more driving, hoping to find a motel near water, trying not to arrive too soon, with too much evening to endure in stillness.

If we stay mainly on interstates, resting at a steady seventy-five, eight hours of sitting eats up six hundred miles. On one day when I could not find a way to stop myself, we made eight hundred. But there are also awful, dead days, when the exhaustion from movement leaves me unable to move at all. America does not seem so big anymore. There's a question as to whether it's big enough, now I know I can go up and down it in a week.

My scarce notes include these: Stratford, Pheasant Capital of Texas; Cassody, Kansas, Prairie Chicken Capital of the World; Atlantic, Coca-Cola Capital of Iowa. This is what strikes me as worth noting.

I'm completely still. It's my midday lie-down. I'm lying wrapped up on a picnic table in a state park with a lake. There's a chill in the air. The park is officially still closed for winter. Arthur is free to roam, which he does, returning to me at intervals, just to make sure. When I open my eyes, I look up through the branches of a leafless tree into a gray sky. I'm sure this place is charming and lively in summer, with green grass leading down to the water.

An ethereal waitress in Tennessee stares over her notepad and out the window of a crummy, dirty diner at my Jeep, offering, wistfully,

"Nice truck," seeming to mean, Please get me out of here. "Thanks," I reply, in the way I've learned in America, to take compliments about possessions as personal. It's a chance against being alone—the only one I've had—but I can't do anything with women anymore and I keep myself to the single word.

I'm looking for a park for Arthur, when the county road ahead leading into a Texas farm town is made uncharacteristically colorful, ragged, and narrow by a demonstration. This road has long had no traffic but me, but the demonstrators are lively and young—the high school probably—smiling and waving their placards as if I was expected. The signs say, on close inspection, that they are against abortion. They have no doubt at all that this will meet with my uncomplicated approval. In spring, a young person's fancy turns to . . . banning abortion. How can this be a natural thing for teens, rather than the more traditional interests: romance, sex, cars, drink, drugs, rock-and-roll? Or, if looking for high ideals to tax the parents, why not poverty, racism, war, the environment. Or even free love. But these teens, who are smiling and waving as I drive slowly among them—Arthur all perplexed attention at the window—are making their stand on a matter of the human soul, its definition, a matter disputatiously philosophical and theological, and surely unsuited to their inexperience. I offer a thumbs down, and the smile on a pretty girl fades to incomprehension, as if I'd slapped her. Arthur, leaning out among all this unaccustomed disorder, finally cannot resist the outbursting of round, deep bark—rare for him, and impressive—so that the placards jump back from us, and we're out of there. "Nice job, boy," I offer.

Men in pickup trucks approaching on these country roads lift a hand, or part of one, from the wheel in greeting, as if I already belong. I'm back in Africa, for some reason, another place where rural greetings are obligatory. There, a wave must always have a smile with it. Here the custom is to never smile. I know why I'm back in Africa—it was the demonstration, reminding me of one I drove into in northern Nigeria in my twenties, which I also did not comprehend. The demand then was for Moslem laws, wanting their religion to be stricter and with more legal force to bind them—not so different really. It had seemed ridiculous at the time, but a quarter of a century later the fundamentalism there has won and strict Moslem law now takes limbs and lives.

The name of a dozy truck stop waitress is Kickapoo. Taken with it, I write down the name and that she is dozy. It's the name of a tribe, it turns out.

This town has two water towers, one labeled hot, one cold. The Indian-owned motel is satisfactory, with a jolly wife in her sari behind the desk, stuck out here on the prairie. It's a joke, she explains, of the water towers. One Indian family per town seems to be the rule across the middle of America. One day someone in a city will tweak the continental web of Indians, and cause myriad new businesses to bloom across the nation's empty center.

A family of four in the family restaurant booth next to me, parents and two teens, completely fill the available space, shoulder to shoulder, bottom to bottom, the fully upholstered family, overstuffed for comfort. They are silent but for heavy breathing, a pleasing weight about them. Resting between their forearms the enormous truck-stop breakfasts—piles of eggs, bacon, sausage, and home fries, glued into place with cheese and slathered with gravy, toast on the side—don't look so enormous. I am trying to observe whether the family members breathe together as one, or alternate. They speak little and there's an enviable comfort in their size and slowness. All through America's depopulating middle the choice for body type has been oversized, as if those remaining feel personally responsible for filling the vacated space.

I write down "James Shield," and "Carrollton." There's a statue of him in the town square of Carrollton, Missouri. Do I think for a moment that I'm making a study of American history?

To get to our room, Arthur and I must pick our way over the legs of the bikers who are sitting on the floor of the corridor, leaning up against the walls, drinking beer. Arthur's good at this, his dainty puppy skills with cattle grids in New Mexico coming in useful. I have to concentrate hard, not well able to lift my feet from the ground, or balance, after a day's driving, and feeling that if I fail my explanation might be too long to be useful. It's a Harley convention and we're the only nonbikers here. They are very polite. All night long they tap on each other's doors, seeking mischief. I remember fun, but it's no longer for me. I believe I am the only one in this hotel injecting himself with vitamin B12 and immunoglobulin.

The gist of this magazine article is that identical twins separated at birth end up with very similar lives. They can grow up in different countries, in very different families, and still dress almost the same, pick similar spouses, have heart attacks at the same time, and possess the same little tics, like flushing the toilet before urinating. I've felt compelled to spend a whole morning at an interstate McDonald's reading this, though it's a long time since I read anything serious. There's relief in it, I suppose, the idea that we have no choice in what we become. If I am genetically programmed to migrate at forty-three, fall ill at forty-four, be on the road without a home at forty-nine, a burden of responsibility is lifted from me, particularly regarding the question of what happens next. It will all happen anyway. If I have an identical twin somewhere, he's in the same fix. My job is not to make the next decision but to have my genes reveal it to me. Just relax. I try this immediately upon leaving the McDonald's, until the car behind me honks at my failure to choose left or right.

The voice is hard and bitter, and it fixes in me. I've finished my recorded books, and I've been searching the radio dial for words, stories preferably. There aren't many, but here's one. It's told in the second person: "You work hard," it tells me. "You try to bring your children up right." Well, that "you" is not really me, but I'll bear with it. "You look after your daddy's farm the way he did. You stay faithful to your wife. You go to church." I can sort of imagine myself that way, a simple, good man. But then I lose my ranch to the banks and the government and I have to go to the city to work in a factory. My wife takes a supermarket checkout job to make ends meet. My kids come under bad influences and don't respect me anymore. The neighbors don't like my big belt buckle or my farm dog. Injustice and lack of respect are all around me. The bitterness in the voice is picking up anger. I go back home to take a look at the old family farm, taking my son to show him, and damn, if it isn't broken up by a developer into ranchettes. Ranchettes! And who owns my land now? City types in SUVs, sipping at their lattes. Well, I'm riled up, and I've slowed down a bit to pay attention, before I sense that we're heading for God and guns, and heading against, well, people like me, who thinks government programs are the right way to manage the pain of economic transition. I shouldn't have let this happen, my engagement with the emotions of the story. Anger burns resources faster than anything, and I'm so shaky now that I'll need to end the day early.

A single bright spot of blood shines on Arthur's upper lip. He's covered in mud, exhausted, his head lolling. The posture is appeasing, yet unapologetic, as if he's certain it would be better for me too to enjoy his adventure, rather than, say, berating him for disappearing for an hour. Probably, I should not have let him loose in this forest, which might be a sort of nature reserve. But it took a long time to find a forest after the hours of Illinois farmland, and by the time we did, Arthur believed he was owed a return to the wild. Running in circles of increasing diameter and speed, nose to the ground, he was off like a slingshot in his chosen direction. I could only wait. I now instruct him to concentrate for the next few days on his lovable, domestic side. His tongue finds the spot of blood and erases it.

Arthur and I have forced our way to the shore of the lake, which is close to the motel, though the motel has chosen to face away from it. He's puzzled as to what to do with it, and so am I. It's an inky, swampy, snaky shore, with tangled trees half in and half out of the water—I'm in Oklahoma, I believe. This lake does not seem healthy, and my blind faith in the healing power of bodies of water is disappointed. I think I had in mind a sunlit Switzerland, a domesticated lake with green pastures leading down to blue water and a luxurious hotel nestled on the shore, cool mountain peaks above it.

I am approaching the East Coast little by little, but apparently I am reluctant to run out of America.

There's a bent pole with a little interstate shield on it, the number concealed by spray paint. Before I reach it, I've drifted into a city without meaning to, first suburbs, shops, and gathering traffic—it must be a Saturday night—then an African American neighborhood with few lights and bad road surfaces, then an abandoned area, old docklands perhaps, with boarded up buildings except for one isolated, barricaded bar, and debris on the street, which could give me a puncture that I would be unable to fix. I have no clue as to which city this is. The neglected, deformed little street sign is the only sign around. After I reach it, taking its cue, I pass between high dark walls, then I am abruptly thrown up into the night sky and onto a busy interstate, riding high and fast above the city, and then onto a bridge across a magnificent river. Saint Louis, I learn from a billboard advertising a radio station.

This town, the newspaper says, is bidding for a prison, which will bring jobs. It's been a common story in small-town papers across the country. Absently, I check out the real estate section. Something is wrong here. I've got used to house prices of forty or fifty thousand and sometimes as low as twenty. In some depopulating farm towns they print no asking prices so as not to shame the sellers. But here the prices are in the hundreds of thousands. I check to see where I am: Milford, Pennsylvania. Through the cafe window, it looks like an ordinary sort of place, the street messy with dirty, unthawed snow. Then I look at the map and I get it. New York City is less than a hundred miles away. That's the reason. I've come perilously close to the East Coast. It's frightening to think of running out of America before I'm ready.

The only movement is the liver-spotted hand of an old man, which is lying palm up on a table, like a small animal. Regularly, every few labored breaths, it flickers over and back, as if trying to return to life. Neither he nor his companions seem to notice. The two elderly couples are the only other customers in the diner and none of us is talking. One of the women did start to tell about how they had installed three RV hookups at their home, so that their three grown children could dock there, but the other woman cut her short with, "Emily, you've told us that a dozen times." There are two RVs parked outside which must belong to them. The men look as tired as I am; in retirement they have chosen to become long distance truck drivers. We are the road dead. I've dragged myself over from the Motel 6 where I have been lying immobile for days. I need to eat. Every time I crash, I lose pounds of weight whether I eat or not, my body consuming itself in its attempts to set things right. What's good about a Motel 6 is their tolerant dog policy. But this one's been grim, next to a loud interstate, surrounded by a wire fence, the ceiling of my room grimly stained, though not in a diverting way. There, it's done it again, the hand, still trying for something.

I've met someone who knows someone I know. This is deeply, deeply shocking. It is completely unexpected, that my earlier London life could reach into this life and tap me on the shoulder. The brother of the Indian woman who runs this motel in upstate New York owns the shop in my old London neighborhood where I used to buy my stationery and do my photocopying. I remember him well. She's excited, insisting that I talk to him when I return to London. I have to tell him about her motel. She's a modern diasporic Indian woman, like the ones I knew in London, like my ex-girlfriend and her family, but especially like Marcella, my invented heroine from Zanzibar. She's cheeky, independent, in her thirties, wearing blue jeans, and like Marcella, she's migrated to America from East Africa via London. I imagined a woman from Zanzibar and left her at an Indian motel in America. And I was right! This one knows her motel is a dive and laughs about it, proof of her belonging to a bigger world.

It is ridiculously thrilling to be reminded that I am connected to the world. England, India, Africa, friends, old neighborhoods, old loves, the unpublished book I've spent five years writing in New Mexico and California, all these are suddenly present for me in a parking lot in upstate New York, chatting with this lively woman, who assumes—and I seem to agree—that I belong in the world just like her. I'm abruptly yanked out from my dazed wandering through the middle of America as if I've been woken from a dream by an electric shock. There is even the glimmer of a new destination and purpose, because I must, she insists, when I get to London—because of course I will be going back to London—visit her family and tell them about her motel and how she's doing. She writes it all down for me. I'm completely at home here, talking to her and exchanging notes in the muddy car park of her dilapidated motel, with its amateur repairs and licks of bright paint.

Lingerie

It's my fiftieth birthday and I'm sleeping on a piece of foam on a cluttered and none too clean floor in Albany. This is not quite what I would have expected for my fiftieth birthday.

When I open them, my eyes are crowded by the backs of canvases leaning against a wall, and a wood floor speckled with drops of oil paint. The painter, Eric, an acquaintance met years ago at an artist colony, has done his best to make this a comfortable bed. Last night I went to a Vietnamese restaurant with his friends and when my birthday was discovered a cupcake and a candle were conjured. Not bad.

What I expected by now was—let's see—a home, a subtle wife, a child or two, a family dog, the tiredness of useful industry, the works of my productive middle period on the shelves, a phone ringing with polite requests from strangers, a self-esteem exactly coinciding with the world's, water nearby, a boat on it or planned for it. The bed would be American-sized and the sleepy, comely body next to mine would from habit migrate toward me, bottom first, seeking warmth and familiarity. The children would, this being my birthday, throw themselves on me and there would be breakfast in bed and presents. All this seemed likely, inevitable, a life course ruled by irresistible currents however much my nature might attempt diversion.

I do, at least, have the dog. Arthur is dozing on the only other available floor space, big head on thick furry forepaws, eyes opening every few seconds—eyebrows quizzical—to check on me, then closing again to check in with the pleasure of dreams, then opening again.

I consider my day before I move and review my body's systems. For no apparent reason I am well. The apartment in an old house is quiet. Eric has gone to his college to teach and it's time for me to be on my way.

Albany could be a place. Property is surprisingly cheap. It's only two hours by train to New York City. I have a friend here—two, actually. Newish friends, it's true, but something to build on. They tell me the city has a funky authenticity. Its charms are not widely known and they expect them to remain so.

The local paper lying next to the toilet confirms the cheapness of property and informs me in a neighboring advertisement that there is a daily lingerie sale. It's ambiguous, but something suggests to me—perhaps its proximity to the personal ads—that the lingerie sale might be cover for something else. I can scent it. The show opens for business at 9 a.m. I'm fifty, alone, have no reputation, nothing at stake, and no remaining pride. I'm on Catastrophic Leave. I decide to check it out on my way east to Vermont, New Hampshire, and Massachusetts, in each of which states I know one person, a realization that makes New England seem crowded with acquaintance.

It's required a hunter's intuition to find this place. I've circled around the marginal industrial areas, the backsides of the low-cost strips and the industrial parks which have lost their industries. And here it is, an incongruous little white cottage at the ragged edge of a wavy tarmac lake on which float big-box discount stores, tire warehouses, and any business where cheapness and quantity trump style and reputation. Finding it has been a quest, as should be any search for love, and having put in the work I cannot now drive away. The cottage has only a modest neon sign in its window—Lingerie—to reveal its purpose, and its ivy-covered decorousness maintains the possibility that this is a place where women discreetly huddle to buy their underwear.

An old-fashioned bell, like the sweetshops of childhood, jingles when I open the door.

"Hello" and "Morning," offer the two smiling young women facing the door, racks of lingerie between them. They are wholesome rather than beautiful, one dressed in jeans, the other in dungarees, little makeup. They've taken minimal trouble over their appearance.
"How can we help you?"
"I'm not sure. You sell lingerie?" There are no other customers.
The shorter one grins and indicates the racks with an ironic sweep of her hand.
"I see," I say.
"Would you like a show?" she asks.
"You could have a private show," confides the other.
They are both laughing, enjoying the ambiguity, sparkling at my discomfort.
"It's forty dollars. That goes to the business, not us."
"OK."
They stand up straight in front of me, like kids, pretending to jostle each other to be chosen for a team. "Who would you like?"
I indicate that it is very difficult to choose, then say to the taller and slimmer, "How about you?" She smiles, the other laughs and offers to catch up on the office work while her friend is busy. These are nice, friendly, funny American girls. I am feeling fine and I don't know what comes next. I'm not thinking about turning fifty.

In the private room she sits me in a chair in front of the sort of bench weightlifters use and goes behind a screen to change. When she emerges the garment is no more revealing than a bathing suit. She twirls.
"You like it?"
"Very pretty."
"They can get more sheer."

“What?”
“Sheer. You know, sheer? You can tip me. It can get really hot.”
She reappears in a one-piece a little more transparent.
“You can make yourself comfortable. We’re very informal here.”
She looks pointedly at my crotch. “Just make yourself comfortable.”
I realize that her conversation is mediated by the fear that it is being recorded.
I put my hand to my belt. “You mean like this?”
She nods. “We can’t quote a price or anything.”
I gave her another forty. “Will this help? I’m new to this.”
From behind the screen she prattles pleasantly. “I’ve never known an Englishman before. I’d love to go there? My neighborhood doesn’t have any immigrants, but the blacks are moving in, you know. Yeah, I’m a student, biology and chemistry. Trying to keep my grades up. Like this?”
This item didn’t cover her breasts or her crotch. She smiles, laughs, sits on the end of bench in front of me. She holds her breasts out toward me, moves her eyes between them and me. I touch and the nipples harden on demand.

She begins to masturbate herself, encouraging me with held eyes and raised eyebrows to do the same. She pushes herself toward me until we are inches apart. “Can I help you?” I say. “Don’t go inside,” she replies, spreading herself. “Snatch shot”—the term comes back to me from the stripper stories of the writing students in San Francisco. Then she is leaning toward me, her hand flickering fast over her clitoris. She kisses me—I had the idea from my students that they never did anything so personal—hands me a tissue. Now she is trying to talk me to climax while she’s working on her own, saying anything that comes into her head: “You’ve got a great stomach. Calvin jeans. I love Calvins. Don’t come on me.” Her own stomach is firm but with a hint of stretch marks. A young mother, I’d guess.

“That was great,” she says, as of course she would. “I think I like the English. We don’t like some of the people we get here. No sense of humor.”

And it has been fun. It has not felt sordid. Somewhere in the middle of America I've lost the inclination to judge. We return to the office area and sit down with the other girl, drinking coffee together. It's still before 11 a.m. and I'm the only customer. "You're a writer? I'm a writing student." The one I had not chosen turns out to be the intellectual. She guilelessly goes off into the shortcomings of the writing program at her college and her teachers, what she likes to read and to write, and what graduate programs would I recommend. Then she teases me when I hesitate to tell her where I teach: "He won't tell us because he's been here." So I tell her, and we talk about that. There is nothing bad about all this. This is just fine. Why had I thought this depraved? I'm just grateful this morning, getting up alone from an acquaintance's grimy floor, that I can find this and buy it. I feel profoundly relaxed and, for the first time for a long time, lucky. I know I have been lucky with these girls, that it need not have been like this.

At last the door bell jingles and a heavy-set man comes in. The girls exchange a grimace, stand up. "I'll leave," I say. "You've got to work. My dog needs a run."

Also, I don't want to see this, the sale of what I've bought.

The one I was with hugs me, and the one I have not been with, the writer, hugs me harder and longer. I leave happy and lifted, and because it has all been so good and welcome, I am sure I will not return. Any love more than this, anything less humble, more generous, or more hopeful, might have broken me.

Massachusetts, 1997–

At Home

It's pleasant here.

My home is, and has been for these last years, a small white Cape in a hamlet on the edge of woods in western Massachusetts. A wood home in the woods. I love this pretty house with its simple proportions, which is, as far as I can determine, two hundred years old, far older than anything I've known in England, and made comfortable over time by the use of others. It's easy too, compact and manageable. I don't need to lock my door. The neighbors up and down the road are friendly and helpful, and in possession of interesting lives. A college town is five miles away, down a winding country road. The next two towns after the first town are also college towns. There are cafes and plenty of artists. The residents are more educated than the average, more considerate, more pacific and ecologic in their politics, and rather shy of proclamations of wealth. Our town halls fly the United Nations flag alongside the American. I'm almost certainly better suited here than in, say, an abandoned Nevada mining town, though this was not at all clear to me when I arrived. Today, in January, tall conifers brush the window of my bedroom, dipping their long branches in homage to the snow, coming close to the crowded bird feeder hanging there. I am a settler, then: this is my American life.

How to Make a Life

First, do not hurry. You cannot seize life; you must wait for it to come to you. This is also the way to befriend dogs and children. While being patient, and refusing to flirt with hope, you make a life without others. It's not a good life, just a life. The only requirement is that it must be rigid enough to support you. Every morning, from the first day of your arrival, you take exactly the same walk with your dog. It will take fifteen to twenty minutes, depending on the ground conditions and how fit you are that day. The route is along a lovely woodland trail close to a brook, which it crosses twice by plank bridges, so as to make a circuit. You invariably walk in an anti-clockwise direction. If finishing the walk is a struggle, it still must be achieved—even if the rest of the day is thereby rendered unpleasant and useless. To fail to finish means you are losing ground and not sustaining a new life. Losing ground is the precursor to giving up, and cannot be entertained. In winter when the plank bridges become humped with ice and too slippery for bipeds, you crawl across rather than fail.

Sometimes you encounter other dog walkers. After a year or so you recognize some regulars and, according to strict etiquette, learn their dogs' names, but not theirs. One dog walker is a woman with two unruly dogs. She always looks like she has thrown on the first old clothes at hand with no regard to appearance, so it takes a while for you to realize she is lovely. At about this time, you also begin to notice that the woodland and the brook are lovely too, and change every day. You notice this only occasionally because your mind is generally caught up in the past with Mary and Zoe. The fact that obsessive thought is not helping you enjoy your new life should arouse your suspicion that you are on the wrong track. But being on the wrong track has become part of your rigid daily habit too.

After the morning walk you add the additional habit of going to a local cafe for coffee and the *New York Times*. For the first two years you go to the wrong cafe and do not talk to anyone. You are in any case dazed into silence by the effort of the walk. In the third year you go to the right cafe, but still do not talk to anyone. By this time the lovely dog walker has become a friend, but she never goes to cafes. It turns out she is a recovering heroin addict working urgently on delayed doctoral research. You are the only one of her friends who is not also a recovering addict; only they can really understand. You discover that you have both done research with the Fulani tribe in West Africa. You discover further that she is the sexually abused child of a father in the military, which is the background to her addiction. You think of the three women in Spokane who you met a decade earlier—a continent ago—in your first months in America, each shot through with the incidental violence of military life. Apparently, you are subconsciously drawn to women with deep, secret hurts, and them to you. You ponder this. Finally, you and the lovely dog walker become close. You are in love again. You are each very tender with the other's hurts.

By the fourth year you think you detect an improving trend in the fluctuations of your health and set about doing more. You talk to someone at the cafe and he leads to other people. One Sunday morning, you throw a breakfast party at your house and invite your new acquaintances, who bring their children and partners, turning them into friends. You've gambled that you will be able to get through the morning without a crash, and you do. Evenings are out of the question.

In the fifth year of your new life, the novel about the woman from Zanzibar that you first completed six years earlier in San Francisco is finally published by a small press. This is the fifth publisher to have been interested in publishing the book, but in the previous four instances the publishers have later reversed themselves for mysterious reasons, as if part of some large plan to inure you to disappointment. In one case a contract is signed and the book is edited and advertised for sale before the publisher bails out. These reversals, like health relapses, have become part of the intrinsic texture of your life. You are being taught how not to hope. But now your book, though earning negligible money, is given a full page in the Sunday Book Review section of the *New York Times* and wins a novel of the year award in San Francisco. At your cafe, you are embraced by some who have always ignored you. You now have a cozy home, a brave lover, a revived career, a dog, some new friends, and a few people to avoid. This may be a life.

It is not, of course, exactly the life you came to America for. You are not enjoying the satisfactions of status and reward that you'd anticipated for your potent middle years. You have not evolved into positions of authority and mentorship. You are not surrounded by entrancing children of various ages, nor do you have an accomplished wife entwined by time into an enduring marital love. Thanks to CFS, you have less status, less affection, less promise, and less money than you possessed on the day you left England for America a decade earlier.

But you do now have this small, new life and sufficient means to support it for a time. What America has delivered to you, in collaboration with illness, is not aspiration realized, nor a largeness of life fitting to its open spaces, but the nascent ability to be satisfied with less. This is not the quality that European visitors generally expect to discover.

Reading in a bookshop from your newly published book, written in the voice of the woman from Zanzibar, you discover her treasuring the small house she lives in on the edge of New England woods, and its age, and the way it has been made comfortable by the use of others. You do not recall writing this. When you wrote it ten years earlier, you were living in an adobe house in a New Mexico village. You did not known then that the contentment you were assigning your imagined immigrant was the one you wanted for yourself.

In the book, the past catches up with the Zanzibari woman in the form of a man who threatens her life. The past catches up with you in the form of suspect and fractured memories, which you write down over eight years, this book, the coincident journey through illness and America.

After years of being together—but living apart—you disentangle from the lovely dog walker. In that time, you have both emerged, in company, from darkness into light, but you both still depend on a rigidity of habit to keep from backsliding. Her condition for the relationship to progress is that you must give up your home, and this proves too much. You finally separate in love, without rancor, and with gratitude, fond friends, family almost. You feel that you have learned in her company something about your difficulties with love that might go into this book. She quickly finds a new man, a doctor, who adores her, and accommodates her, and whom she marries.

You are unattached—though still looking—and you discover that you are unexpectedly . . . all right. Life is no longer desperate with loneliness. You are something close to happiness, and you have some love to offer. You look into adopting a child, before, a year or two later, reluctantly accepting that your persisting health relapses make it impracticable. After all this time, you are still fooled by every remission into believing that it signals permanent recovery. Your health is, in fact, not significantly better, but you now know how to live quietly so as not to make it worse, and you have a place to be still when this is all that is possible.

The Cost of Illness

The cost of my first fifteen years of chronic fatigue syndrome was one million six hundred and twenty thousand dollars. Trust me; I'm an economist.

Or, the equivalent, say, of a million dollar house, a Bentley Continental, and a forty-five-foot sailing yacht equipped for circumnavigation.

Or, the entire cost of comfortably raising a family, including college fees for two and a half children.

Only a fraction of the total cost is directly due to doctors, treatments, and medicine. Most of the cost of CFS is the difference between what I would have earned over the fifteen years and my actual income, and the difference between what remains of my savings and what my savings would now be worth if I had not spent them on living.

I've been lucky. I had a London flat to sell. I had a boat to sell. I had some savings. I had no debts or dependents. My approach to money had been more aligned with English postwar scarcity than with the Californian assumption of abundance. And it turned out that the California job carried disability insurance, a concept new to me, and as awkward as it was welcome, since I was painfully reluctant to count myself among the disabled. The work I do, this writing, can wait until the periods when I am more able, so that as time has passed I have earned a little and, in consequence, given up the disability payments. So far I have managed, but since my living costs far exceed any income, the future is not clear.

Many sufferers from CFS have not had my advantages, many are far more ill, and for them there is only a plunge into wretched poverty to go with the pain, inability and lack of respect.

Lost and Found

It's pleasant here.

When I lie down—as I have for much of the time since I arrived here—it is on my bed with its views of the garden and the birds, or on the daybed downstairs, or on the couch in the upstairs study, or on the futon in the guest room, where I keep the TV. It's a house equipped for horizontal life. And when I am lying down, I sometimes fall into a profound quiet. It has taken these years for my parts to collect and settle. Sometimes, for long periods, I forget that I am foreign.

This home has given me the chance to garden for the first time. I undertake a light, approximate version of gardening, neither intensive nor extensive. But I like the slow collusion with nature. If I plant something today, it will show itself months down the road. I must wait, while it does the work without me. There are no hurry-up possibilities, and there is a good measure of chance, which I do little to reduce. The ratio of time wandering around the garden—or "yard"—this rocky third-acre, to see what is poking up, compared with time actually working in the garden is about ten to one. I know a lot about what is going on out there, but I don't remember many of the names.

My understanding of what has happened to me, this big deviation from my designated path, has settled too, though it is not yet fixed. It's hard not to blame yourself for illness; the earlier life, in retrospect, was full of foolishness and excess. Others prefer blame too, both to excuse themselves from care and to immunize themselves from susceptibility. And there is the seduction of metaphor, with illness so much more interesting than itself when given a moral dimension. I have been firmer correcting others in their suspicion that CFS is self-inflicted or psychological than I have been with myself.

At intervals, over the years, this uneasiness has been fanned by the disability insurance company. If the illness is deemed physical in origin they must pay; if psychological, they need not. From time to time the insurance company has sent me to carefully selected doctors, to try and make the case for the separation of mind and body on behalf of its shareholders. On one occasion this philosophical quest involved providing a limousine to drive me out of state to visit a doctor who once wrote that CFS was a form of depression, though it turned out that he was embarrassed, and had changed his mind.

The intermittent need to prove to doctors that my illness is not in my mind—when clearly my mind is affected—and to prove to the company's private investigators that I am disabled—when every day is taken up by trying to seem not disabled—causes paroxysms of internal conflict.

The mind-body distinction is, of course, insane. From time to time I check up on medical research for CFS and what I discover goes some way to showing just how insane is this proposition. The current preferred name for CFS is myalgic encephalopathy, a mouthful that translates to brain disease with muscle pain, which is fair enough as far as it goes. The essence of the illness seems to be viral damage in the brain, particularly affecting that part of the brain controlling the body's autonomic functions. With all the body's systems now eccentrically regulated, and the brain's activities themselves directly impaired, the cascading symptoms become myriad and unpredictable in the way that customarily frustrates both sufferers and doctors. This science feels right: that mind and body functions are both comprehensively and jointly deranged by shared long-term damage.

Which is only the beginning of understanding, since it does not explain why one person—well, actually one million people in America alone—falls ill and not another. The specific most implicated viruses shift according to the latest medical discoveries, but a general proposition is that the sufferers are those made most susceptible to damage by failures in their immune system. Since the immune system is where the body—the person—mingles with the outside world, this opens up explanation to everything in the world. The flulike illness that preceded my collapse at the Spokane Sta-Fit gym—a typical sequence—is suspected of precipitating a profound immune failure that enabled this chronic viral illness, but many other factors are implicated in an immune system's disposition to fail. Effort, stress, pollutants, pharmaceuticals, heartbreak—all of life, in fact—act to weaken immunity, producing the familiar colloquial condition of being "run down." To this complex of pathogens, environmental conditions and life experiences, there must also be added genetic disposition. We are our experiences, but also everything that has been experienced before us.

It may be that the way I aspire to live today is the way I always should have lived—how everyone should live—if I had wanted to be healthy and content. Now, I am more careful about what I eat and drink and more mindful of the air I breathe, since bad air or the wrong food can trip or speed relapses. Now, I check that my pride is not making me too willful and tense in my effort and ambitions, that my ego does not attempt to override my body. I pay attention to the present state of body and mind, so that I do not push them to the point of a failure. I avoid anger and try for harmony. I try not to be too alone, and try not to stake everything on the risky rewards of one big love. I take pride in being more humble. More patient. I avoid the distractions of excitement, turn my back on violence, and accept that peace comes with favoring concern for others over self-interest. At least that is the aspiration from which I continually fall short.

The knowledge forced on me by the practicalities of CFS is simply the age-old wisdoms of all spiritual traditions, that in a busy life, always focused on the next thing, I might have missed. I've come to appreciate the value of meditation, for the practical reason that its release from busy thought cools the inflamed discomfort in my brain. It seems like sanity. Without illness this would be less clear.

In short, I have had pressed on me by illness the eternal good sense and wisdom of being present in my body, and relaxing the self in something larger. I am, this illness has proved, not divisible within myself, nor separable from without. My borders are permeable, the border patrol flawed and corruptible. The new understanding is that my self is not a knot of self-regard located in my mind, but some large and labile thing existing beyond my full control in a continuum of brain, body, other living beings, and all substance beyond. In short, the nature of CFS is an object lesson in oneness. Which is an object lesson in love. You are lost, yet you are found.

It is strange to have received this understanding in a country where the divisiveness of competition, specialization, and the market cut deepest, where distraction is privileged over attention, where quantity is traditionally favored over quality, noise over silence, and where present contentment is most fervently discounted in favor of the hope of future happiness. On the other hand, judging by my new hometown, with its viral outbreak of health food, meditation, yoga and green living, the ills of America are creating their own immune response.

Doctors

The idea of an illness, and individual health, being inseparable from all existence is generally too fancy for doctors, who have five minutes to listen to a stranger, make a decision, and write a prescription or order up a test. Though CFS is only one of many illnesses of similar complexity—and overall health is always of this complexity—doctors are forced by circumstance into a simpler understanding. This makes them sad, brave and comic, the balance depending largely on how brashly they attempt to cloak their limitations with authority. They live at one remove from reality and one remove from love, and this causes them distress.

I've come to sympathize with doctors, knowing that the new one will be unable to cure me too. Sometimes I accept their treatments only out of politeness. Health care—the social immune system that we clever humans have invented for ourselves while our cleverness has undermined the natural one—is still based on the Victorian science of Koch's postulate. Each disease, Koch proposed in 1884, is caused by a specific microorganism that could be identified by always being present with the infections and never being present without the infection. One disease, one cause, one treatment. It's the basis of the five-minute doctor visit, and the drug rep in the waiting room.

The problem with this proposition is that it was never a sound basis for medicine and proves to be less and less sound with time. Even the areas of medicine that seem most susceptible to a simple approach—have infection; take penicillin—have later proved to lead to false solutions as infective agents mutated into invulnerability and natural immunity was compromised by drugs. Also, oddly, it has been discovered that the same infective agents cause different diseases in different parts of the world, or can express themselves in a bewildering variety of symptoms. The Epstein-Barr virus, believed by Grumpy, my first doctor, to be the cause of CFS, is the decided cause of mononucleosis, but is also implicated in throat cancer, Hodgkin's disease, and Burkitt's lymphoma. Or, as my second doctor, Happy, noted, it can be present in the body with no symptoms at all, in full defiance of Koch's postulate. A pill can rarely do the job. Most illnesses, the currently incurable ones, are complex, with roots in all of life, but medical practice remains stubbornly simple. Strong forces maintain the fiction: insurance companies like the abbreviated doctor visit, and drug companies love the prescription that marks its end. So the fault is repeated, and repeated, and repeated.

An incomplete list of the ingested and tested, compiled from leftover medicine bottles and scraps of medical documentation (no need to read)

Gammaglobulin; Imunovir—inosine pranobex; L. salivarius; dehydroepiandrosterone; Armour Thyroid; Triiodo-1-thryron; Arginine; Cipro; Doxycycline; Carbenicillin; Tmp Smz Ds; 5-hydroxytryptophan; bladder lavage for cytologies; allergen immunotherapy; retrovirus antigen; Ester-C with bioflavonoids; clostridium difficile toxin; chromium; liver tonic; ginko; ginseng (three types); Vermex; infusion therapy; Zocor; vitamin therapy; co-enzyme Q10; vitamin D3; Captomer (DMSA); C-Max; Florinef; cortisol; Wellbutrin; Celexa; Lipitor; chelation therapy; cyanocobalamin; lactose powder; immune globulin; syringes; Chlorella; human growth hormone; human USP gamma; NADH; Famvir; folic acid; niacin; Chromium Aspartate; Pantethine; Vanadium; vitamin E; L-Carnitine; taurine; Chinese herbs; St. John's wort; acupuncture needles; Cortef; papaya enzyme; IC hydrocodone/apap; green tea extract; Miacalcin; Reishitaki; Serodex; Amebex; oscillo liq.; Spirulina; Diptherium; Thymetabs; royal jelly; medorrhinum; miso soup; Pulsatilla; Effexor; vitamin B12; Pravachor; Vita Biotic; Opti Biotic; Policosanol plus Gugulipid; chlorpheniramine maleate; Zoloft; spirolena; zinc; adrenal cortex extract; Scut 200 homeopathic medicine; Pic-ac 0/3; homeopathic medicine; Thermotabs; Lexapro; magnesium; fish oil (*cont.*).

Tests: Epstein-Barr titer; mono test; CBC add-on; amoeba antibody; magnesium (RBC); Epstein-Barr virus AB panel; free cortisol rhythm; antibody, Lyme disease, lipid profile, chem 8, glutamyl-transferase, gamma-CGT; DHEA; PSA; HDL W/CALC; CBC/Platelet; urine culture-colony count; urine culture ID first organism; echography, retroperiotoneal; echography, pelvic; abdomen, single AP view; blood chemistry panel; Hemoccult; PPD; EKG; thyroid stimulating hormone; urinalysis; sedimentation rate (ERS); anti-nuclear bodies (ANA); microsomal antibodies; thyroglobulin antibody; urography; stool culture; CBC; SMAC; WBC differential; Candix; EBV Capsid Ab; EBV early AG; EBV nuclear AG; animal mix; smears, routine gram stain; pathogenic Neisseria screen; reticulocyte count; urine aluminium, arsenic, beryllium, lead, nickel, creatinine, cadmium, mercury; uric acid; rheumatoid factor; cystoscopy; panendoscopy; hemogram; testosterone; DHEA—S; urine cytology; anti-HIV antibody test; prostate specific antigen; RBC mag.; RBC zinc; methylmalonic acid serum; lymphocyte transformation; B1-thiamin; B2-riboflavin; B6-pyridoxine; B12-cobalamin; folate; calcium; asparagine; glutamine; serine; oleic acid; glutathione; cysteine; gammaglobulin, IGA, D, G, M, each; iron; triglycerides; hemoglobin, glycated; thyroid stimulating hormone; free thyroxine; TSH; free T; EBV VCA IgG; EBV VCA; amoebic AB-CF IgM; IgG cytomegalovirus; IgM cytomegalovirus; IgG herpes; IgM herpes; cortisol; electrolyte balance; food test provocation for wheat, egg, corn, milk, histamine, yeast, soy; sodium; potassium; chloride; glucose; creatinine; osmolarity; albumin; phosphorus; bilirubin; urea; mold screen; SET screen; giardia-specific antigen (EIA); cytoporidium immunofluorescence; sinus rhythm; RAST tests (*cont.*)

The Benefits of Illness

Your choices are limited
And therefore easier.

Small achievements are automatically promoted to big ones.

You save on shoe leather.

Any woman interested in you is likely to be nice
Though you hope not too nice.

Unpleasant women stay away from you
Though some are confused as to their category.

You learn a lot about the behavior of birds at your bird feeder.

Your illness drives away those frightened by the fragility of life
That is, most men.

You are always home for parcel deliveries.

You keep up with the world news.

Your week never need be empty
While there are doctors to visit.

You watch many films, often twice
Since you forget.

The quality of patience is not strained
Since it's unavoidable.

Your dog need not feel inferior to you
Since you lie down with him.

You appreciate for the first time the pleasures of gardens.

You receive sympathy
Though actually not that much.

You no longer become angry
Because it makes you sick.

You are freed from ambition
Because it makes you sick.

You avoid heartbreak
Because it makes you sick.

You know yourself inside out.

Spiritual wisdom is forced on you
Again and again and again.

You become a connoisseur of repose.

You are motivated to think of others
Since you are so tired of yourself.

You can go to bed in the afternoon
Without a moment's guilt.

You are as sensitive to the air
As is a sailor to the wind.

You have the space and time to daydream.

You always possess a perfect excuse
Though you do not use it
Since there is no end to that.

Permission to Be Human

America is at war again, in Iraq again, as it was when I first fell ill. The reservists have it worse this time, the families split longer and hurt deeper than the tearful ones I first saw in Spokane. The chance of death and injury—receiving and inflicting—is greater and the justifications for all this suffering more spurious. The damage of violence will be lodged in them and will reach down through the generations.

I've received a great deal of kindness in America, and most of this has been from women. Care is not easy for the men. In California, as a new resident, sick and overworked, I found myself driving a man to his regular cancer treatments. In his sixties, he was living alone and had many sportsman pals, but no one else had stepped forward. Sick men are both embarrassed for themselves and embarrassing to other men. Caring is thought womanly, and the fear of feminine traits is strong. Illness, it seems to be thought, as a warrior ideal, should be susceptible to manly will. Acceptance is taken to be a sort of weakness, its acknowledgment as whining. Men, short on love and community, seek help less readily, suffer more serious illnesses, die earlier.

While America loses its friends, savings, authority, there is a scent of something familiar to me in the air, cozy almost, of a grandeur no longer affordable, of inevitable, natural decline. It's exactly the scent I grew up with in postwar England. It's not unpromising.

I've heard, now and then, from the first people I met in my new American life, the last ones before I fell ill, the three kind women in Spokane each with army violence in her. Brilliant Carol, last heard of, had given up her teaching career before it started and was working in the office of a small-town trucking company, back home, hooked up with a lowlife. Krissy broke her Russia contract early, reflexively tricking superiors according to the lessons of her military career, by feigning pregnancy. She brought a young Russian man back with her and asserted the authority of love. Marianne fought authority at colleges across the middle of America, then attempted suicide, then magnificently picked herself up in her sixties to become a labor leader in a tractor factory. My farmer friends, Jack and Clara, in New Mexico, whose romantic return to the land made me anxious about a destitute old age, inherited old money and bought a Rolls-Royce.

Last heard of, Mary was still in California. According to the news her father gave me, Zoe was at a good university.

In recent years my periods of relative health have seemed longer, and the relapses shorter, and I've tried to do more. I am unsure how much of this is an improvement in my condition and how much an improvement in my skill in managing it. Twice I made carefully orchestrated visits to Northeast India for an old Indian friend at a UN agency, to oversee making a documentary film, lying down on a new continent. The effort teased me with the restoration of a larger, more useful life, but it was also a variety of hell to be in a remote place, with responsibilities, and a mind and body that would not work.

When I persuaded myself that I was recovering, I looked seriously into adopting a child, and my American friends said, yes, go for it, we'll help you, while my English friends told me not to be ridiculous, sensibly pointing out the difficulties with health, wealth, and age. I have not been ridiculous, but I also have not adopted a child. I liked America for the yes. I've become a citizen, with a vote in the place where I live.

Arthur died, a sudden death while I was away from home in connection with the documentary film. He'd stayed with me that far, until I'd made something of a new life, until I was able to travel again. He was staying with a family he liked and reportedly took a vigorous morning run in the woods before lying down to die an hour later. Eleven years, neither long nor short for a big dog's life. The vet could not discover any cause. His life was, of course, blameless. Without intent, he brought pleasure to countless people, lying outside the local cafe, offering his belly to strangers, welcoming the rough embraces of children, taking fear away from the timid ones. He was an animal who gave humans permission to be more human. Always eager, never dismayed for long, huge in heart and stomach, he reigned over the woodland paths for his last seven years, king of the dogs—at least to his own understanding—magnificently oblivious in age to any upstart challenge to his eminence. In New England he discovered squirrels for the first time, his natural foils, never catching one, but successfully firing them vertically daily, like rockets, all celebrated with shameless swagger. He trusted me completely—even through the agony of plucking porcupine quills from the inside of his mouth—was never sure where he ended and I began, and was not unhappy with this erosion of identity. He was born, made happiness without meaning to, died.

The End

Acknowledgments

Without the relief from worldly effort offered by fellowships at the MacDowell Colony, the Virginia Center for the Creative Arts, and the Corporation of Yaddo, this book would not have been written.

I owe many debts to friends and writers who have kept me going and put me straight. Any list would fall short, and I hope they know who they are. Andrew Blauner and Elizabeth Kurtz of the Blauner Books Literary Agency stayed the distance and stayed charming. My sincere thanks to them. Raphy Kadushin, my brave editor at the University of Wisconsin Press, had faith, and without exception, the warm, efficient people at UWP give publishing a good name. Finally, in a class of her own, I thank Michelle Aldredge for all she does and all she is.